It penetrated her sleep and open door, silhouetted in th

Whomp-whomp-whomp.

Realization dawned. A helicopter. Someone to rescue them.

Newfound energy surged through Sylvie, and she ran to Will on her injured ankle. "Why aren't you out there signaling them?" She pushed by, prepared to limp outside. "If you won't, then I will."

"Sylvie, no." He gripped her shoulders, his eyes imploring her to listen. "The help I radioed for won't be here for hours." He nodded toward the helicopter. "That's not our help."

She froze. "What are you saying?"

"I'm saying that could be the men after you."

She backed away from him. "No, that can't be. How–"

A spray of bullets ricocheted through the woods. Will slammed the door and pressed his back against it. Determination was carved into his features. "We have to get out of here."

A chunk of fear lodged in her throat. When would this end? She knew the answer...and that was what scared her.

Elizabeth Goddard is an award-winning author of over twenty novels, including the romantic mystery *The Camera Never Lies*—winner of a prestigious Carol Award in 2011. After acquiring her computer science degree, she worked at a software firm before eventually retiring to raise her four children and become a professional writer. In addition to writing, she homeschools her children and serves with her husband in ministry.

Books by Elizabeth Goddard

Love Inspired Suspense

Mountain Cove

Buried
Untraceable
Backfire
Submerged
Tailspin

Freezing Point
Treacherous Skies
Riptide
Wilderness Peril

Visit the Author Profile page at Harlequin.com.

TAILSPIN

ELIZABETH GODDARD

HARLEQUIN® LOVE INSPIRED® SUSPENSE

Recycling programs
for this product may
not exist in your area.

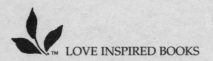 LOVE INSPIRED BOOKS

ISBN-13: 978-0-373-44735-0

Tailspin

This edition published by arrangement with Love Inspired Books.

® and TM are trademarks of Love Inspired Books, used under license.
Trademarks indicated with ® are registered in the United States Patent
and Trademark Office, the Canadian Intellectual Property Office and in
other countries.

www.Harlequin.com

Printed in U.S.A.

But they that wait upon the Lord shall renew their strength;
they shall mount up with wings as eagles; they shall run,
and not be weary; and they shall walk, and not faint.
                        —Isaiah 40:31

To my Lord and Savior, Jesus Christ,
who truly does renew my strength.

Acknowledgments

When it comes time to write acknowledgments, there are so many people I want to thank. Too many to name in a short paragraph, but all my heartfelt gratitude goes to my family—my parents and grandparents who encouraged me, always telling me that I could be whatever I wanted to be. They taught me the sky was the limit. To dream as big as I wanted to dream and accomplish even more. The journey to this place of living my dream of writing novels has taken years, and it's a journey I would never have made without God, who continued to nudge and direct me to answer His call. Along the way I've made many deep and lasting friendships—my partners in writing and in life. You know who you are. Thank you. I want to thank my wonderful editor Elizabeth Mazer, for your encouragement and suggestions that make my books the best they can be. I could never forget my amazing agent, Steve Laube. Thank you for believing in me.

ONE

The scuba-diving dry suit, along with the warm layers beneath, protected Sylvie Masters from the biting cold waters of the channel that carved its way through the Alaska Panhandle.

Breathe too fast, you could die. Hold your breath, you could die. Stay too long, you could die. Ascend too fast, tiny little bubbles of nitrogen on a death mission enter your bloodstream.

Her mother's words, an effort to dissuade her from her love of scuba diving, gripped her mind as she searched for the missing plane in the depths. Her mother had worried about Sylvie's diving, but in turn, Sylvie had reminded her that famous undersea explorer Jacques Cousteau had lived to be eighty-seven, his death unrelated to his underwater endeavors, and his sons were still alive except the one who died in a plane crash—a seaplane, no less!

Sylvie never imagined her words would be so prophetic. Never imagined that horrible phone call two months earlier, telling her that a seaplane with her mother on board had disappeared without a trace, and that her mother was missing and presumed dead.

A sea lion glided past, much too close for comfort, and Sylvie exhaled sharply, her pulse accelerating. The enormity of the creature this close left her in awe. The large mammal, intent on a search of his own, swam away, putting a comfortable distance between them.

Slowing her breathing, she flutter-kicked and moved on. The glint of painted metal, something completely unnatural to the environment, caught her attention. A wing thrusting from the sandy bottom? The final resting place for a plane and passengers?

Her heart jumped, taking her breathing with it. Not good. At two atmospheres, or forty feet, this was a simple recreational dive. But she still needed to maintain slow, steady breaths. Two cardinal rules: never overbreathe and never hold your breath.

Inhale...

Exhale...

Her body was like a carbonated drink. The deeper the dive, the harder the shake. She only had to remember to open the bottle slowly, ascend at the proper rate with the right stops and then, upon surfacing, her body wouldn't explode with nitrogen bubbles like a shaken can of soda opened too quickly. She wouldn't get decompression sickness.

The bends.

As an instructor for a diving school in Seattle, and a volunteer member of a local dive rescue organization, Sylvie had ample experience and was trained to solo dive. Good thing, too. Chelsey, a friend at the school, had planned to come with her, but Chelsey's sister was seriously injured in a car wreck the day before they were to leave, and she needed to be at her sister's side. Sylvie didn't blame her for that, but neither would she wait until Chelsey could join her for yet another search for her mother's missing plane.

She'd already taken the vacation time. It was late September, and the water would soon get colder with winter. It was now or never. Besides, she wasn't sure she wanted to drag anyone else with her on what could be a morbid discovery.

Six weeks ago the powers-that-be had given up on ever finding the plane, but Sylvie would never stop.

She pushed her thoughts back to the present and her task. More fish darted past, drawing her gaze from the metal for only a moment. She loved the water and all its inhabitants. Her mother had always told her she should have been born a dolphin or a whale, some sort of sea mammal. Just give Sylvie the ocean any day as long as she didn't have to fly.

Because the cold water was clearer, she could see much farther than on a warm-water dive. She spotted the remnants of an old shipwreck, which had created an artificial reef for cold-water sea creatures. Brightly colored starfish and anemones in every shade of pink and green mesmerized her, reminding her of everything she loved about diving.

Except she wasn't here to enjoy the scenery this time.

She was on a mission and had been for the past several days. And she'd found nothing, seen nothing, until now. In the distance, she could still see the glint of metal, and needed to keep her focus on that or she might lose it.

Excitement and dread swirled together and gurgled up in her stomach, much like the bubbles escaping from her regulator and swirling around her head on their way to the water's surface. She kicked her fins furiously, hoping to find what she was looking for. When a shadow moved over her from above, she noted another boat on the water coming or going, crossing over her despite her diver down flag, but she kept going.

Something grabbed her fin and tugged.

Sylvie turned around and faced another diver, who wielded a glinting diver's knife and lunged. Her mind seized up. Survival instincts kicked in. He could fatally wound her, or go for her hose, hold her down and drown her. Kill her a million different ways. She turned and tried to swim away.

But he caught her fin again.

Sylvie faced her attacker. Murderous dark eyes stared back at her from behind a diver's mask. She couldn't swim her way out of this. She'd have to fight her way free. She struggled but he was physically stronger.

She'd have to be smarter. She could hold her breath longer than most, though holding her breath could kill her, too.

Help me, Lord!

His knife glinted in the water. Sylvie kicked and thrashed to get away, bumping up against sharp coral that ripped a hole in her dry suit and a gash in her back. Frigid water rushed through the hole in the suit. She ignored the shock of cold biting her skin and the salty sting of her wound.

The crazed diver whipped the knife around and sliced through her regulator hose.

Sylvie flailed and swam for the surface, but he dragged her back.

This couldn't be happening.

Who was this man? What did he want? The next few

moments could be her last. Sylvie fought, but fisted against water, flailed and then…relaxed.

Dead.

The man released his hold on her.

Now.

Sylvie yanked the hose from his tanks. While he struggled with his own breathing apparatus, she ditched her weight belt and thrust her way to the surface. She released air from her lungs with a scream and tried to ascend at a controlled pace, which would also expand the air in her lungs as she released it instead of having them pop like balloons. If this worked, she wouldn't be unconscious by the time she reached the surface.

He wouldn't be fooled twice.

When Sylvie breached the water, she dragged in a long breath. A boat rested a few hundred yards from her, but it wasn't her boat. Treading water, she searched the area. Her boat was gone. Panic rose like a fury in her throat, and she stifled the frustrated scream that would surely alert whoever was left on the boat, waiting for the diver who'd come to kill her.

She had to hurry. He'd be up and after her soon enough. She'd only delayed him long enough to make a temporary escape.

But where should she hide? In this part of Alaska, she was surrounded by islands and trees, and trees and islands, and oh yeah, rain. A slow drizzle started up— of course—pock-marking the water around her. With no other choice, she headed to the scrap of land that barely passed for an island.

Could she make it there before the boat ran her down or the diver caught up to her?

* * *

Will Pierson couldn't imagine living any other way. He was an eagle soaring over the awe-inspiring landscape of southeast Alaska. Okay, so he wasn't an eagle. He was a simple bush pilot sitting in a tin can, bouncing and twisting and riding the rough air to deliver packages or people to the Alaskan bush.

And today, while he did his job, he searched for his mother's plane like he'd done every day since she'd crashed.

He flew low, swooping over a forgotten part of God's green earth, waters of the channel shimmering in the cold morning sun, what there was of it. His Champ 7GC glided over green and misty islands and jaw-dropping fjords. He often looked down to see the wildlife, maybe a few off-grid pioneer-types, sometimes bear or elk.

As he soared over the wide-open spaces, he admitted the joy he found in the view was overshadowed by loss and grief.

His mother, the packages and one additional passenger had disappeared, and no one knew exactly where or even why. It wasn't as if their bush pilot planes were big enough to warrant cockpit voice recorders or flight data recorders or the "black boxes" carried by commercial planes. And out here in the Alaska bush, they flew without radar coverage for the most part. Investigators had suggested that she'd been flying below clouds in poor visibility and slammed into the ground or the side of a mountain. He refused to believe it. As a bush pilot flying southeast Alaska for the past two decades, she knew the area too well.

Since that day two months ago, Will had flown a thousand times over the area where her plane should have gone down. He tried to trust God to give him the peace he longed for, but his need to know what had happened drove him crazy. Surely he owed her that much— a decent burial and a clear understanding of what had caused her death.

She'd taught him to survive. Alaska was about survival of the fittest. She'd taught him to spread his wings and fly above the storms of life like an eagle. In this way, they had survived his father's brutal scuba-diving death and built a solid life for the two of them that had lasted until the day she'd gone to pick up a surprise package she'd said was going to shake things up. Well, things had been shaken all right, and his mother was dead and gone.

She was a skilled pilot. Something must have gone wrong with the plane. Equipment failure? Or worse. Had one of the packages been a bomb?

The thought made Will edgy with every trip he took. Every package he picked up or delivered. He didn't want any surprise packages. He just wanted answers.

His Champ hit a rough spot, a pothole in the air as he liked to call it.

And that was when he saw someone running.

She was not out for a jog wearing a diving suit. That much he could tell. She looked as if she was running for her life. Will flew in close, sweeping the area, and searched. Was she running from a bear? The woods were thick around the meadow where she ran. Where was she heading? She was too focused on her escape to glance at his plane swooping low. He didn't have to get any closer to see she had terror written all over her face.

And then Will saw him.

A man with a rifle. Will took a dive, letting the

guy know he should back off. Between the trees, the man appeared to gaze through his scope at Will. He backed away, lifted higher and out of range. But not fast enough. He heard the ping of a bullet against the fuselage.

Will tried to radio for help, but to no avail, which was just as he'd expect out in this part of southeast Alaska. No one on the other end of his radio call answered to help this woman, so that meant he would have to do. Even if he had reached someone for help, what were the chances they would arrive in time? Zero.

He was on his own.

But how could he help her? He swung around the small island to come back and find the best place to land on the water, hoping she would see him. Hoping the rifleman wouldn't.

Right. That was going to work.

Will sucked in a breath and veered wide and plunged low, coming around to find the woman. He'd seen a boat anchored nearby. Was that hers? Or the rifleman's? Somehow he had to intervene and get her out before the man got to her. Flying low over the thick trees, he couldn't see either one of them.

But he needed to keep his distance, too. Bad enough the man was shooting at someone—and Will wouldn't stand idly by and let that happen without a fight—but if his plane was badly damaged then both Will and the woman would have nowhere to turn, no way to escape.

How could he let her know he was friendly and not with the hunter? And how could he find her at all? She'd dropped completely out of sight. Had she found a place to hide in the woods? Or…was she headed for the water? She wore a diving suit, after all.

He prayed this would all end well as he made for the water somewhere near the direction she'd been headed. Then he could offer her a ride home.

Will maneuvered his floatplane onto the water. This was cutting things close.

The pontoons touching down, he proceeded forward, watching the rough edges and sandy beaches where the land met water and the rocky outcroppings, searching for the woman and the rifleman. Both of them could be heading away from him for all he knew. Or they could be moving straight for him through the island rainforest of the Tongass National Forest. As he steered closer, Will found his weapon and placed it on the passenger seat.

Closing in on the island, he slowed the plane. A slow burn worked its way up his gut as he took the plane right up to a small section of sand, remaining wary of the thick forest hidden with danger. Which one of them would he see first?

The woman, running for her life?

Or the man with his rifle, aiming to kill?

TWO

Fear drove her past the pain of her injuries, through the shock of it all. Sylvie pushed her body because her life depended on it. Grateful for the diving boots she'd worn under her fins to protect her feet, she ran from another madman, this one holding a high-powered rifle instead of a diver's knife.

If she could just make it to the water.

Again.

Hard to believe she'd escaped the crazy diver beneath the surface only to face off with another dangerous man. This wasn't some random meeting, but an elaborate plan to assure her death.

She could almost laugh at their efforts—how hard had they believed she would be to kill?

Her legs screamed, and she stopped to lean against a Sitka spruce, catching her breath. The dry suit hadn't been designed for running.

At first she'd thought the plane was just another part of the plan. A diver. A man with a rifle. Why not a floatplane to attack her in some other, horrible way? But then the man who'd been there to give her an unfriendly welcome as she dragged her body from the water onto the rocky shore had taken a few shots at it.

Providence had sent someone to save her in the most inappropriate manner. God had a sense of humor. Why couldn't it be another boat? Why not the Coast Guard? She would never fly unless she had no choice.

But then Sylvie had never needed saving before.

And now that floatplane that had flown low and deep to find her running, and had made waves for her would-be killers, meant everything to her. She assumed the plane waited just beyond the trees. She'd seen that much—but unfortunately that meant the rifleman had seen it, as well.

Breathing hard and fast, Sylvie pushed through the wildness of this uninhabited land, brushing past thick and lush sword ferns and alongside a thorny undergrowth that shredded her dry suit. Through the trees she could make out the water.

She continued on to the water's edge and searched for the plane. Down from her a few hundred yards, the plane waited. The whir of the props echoed across the water. Her stomach lurched. Would he leave before she could get there? How could she signal him to wait? Draw his attention without giving away her position?

God, please let him wait for me! Help me!

It was too far for her to quickly traverse the thick brush and rocky shore, but there was another way. Sylvie rushed into the water and dove beneath the surface, quickly reminded of the brush against the coral during her struggle with the mad diver. Her dry suit no longer protected her from the cold water that seeped in, icing across her skin and into her bones, it seemed, slowly stealing her body heat away.

Hypothermia would set in soon. Never mind her aching joints that brought to her attention another problem. Sylvie was too experienced to ignore the symptoms or write them off as the shock of nearly being brutally murdered.

No. She had to face the truth.

She had the bends. Decompression sickness.

But she had to keep it together until she made it to the plane. Holding her breath, she swam just under the water's surface to keep out of sight. Without her mask, her eyes burned in the salty water as she remained vigilant in watching for the boat and the man with the rifle. She prayed the other diver wasn't right behind her.

The flash of an image rushed at her—the diver's knife, glinting in the water as he cut her hose. Shivering, she tossed a quick look into the depths behind and beneath her. She had to be sure the diver wasn't closing in. At least she was safe for the moment. Head bobbing to the surface for a quick breath, she continued to swim, her limbs growing sluggish.

She drew near to the plane.

Almost there.

The pilot scrambled from the plane and onto the beach, brandishing a weapon. Her pulse quickened. Could that be for her? *God, please let him be friendly. Please let him be someone here to help me.* She didn't know what she would do otherwise.

Dizziness swept over her, swirling through her core with the shock of the last few minutes.

But Sylvie was strong. She couldn't have excelled in her career as a diving instructor if she wasn't.

Then she heard it.

The echoing fire from a rifle. Sylvie ducked under

the water. Had the rifleman seen her? Was he firing at her now in the water? Or at the pilot?

She was cold and numb and drained. Wasn't sure she could breach the surface again. She heard the rumble of the floatplane before she found the energy to bob above the water's surface and see it moving.

Disappointment weighed her down into the depths.

The rifleman was shooting at her rescuer. If he'd come to help, he'd been scared away. Sylvie fought the desire to give up, to sink and keep on sinking. Anger burned in her chest along with the need for air.

No, God! Her life couldn't end like this.

Like her mother, Sylvie was a fighter, and she'd find a way to survive this. There were a million reasons to live, not the least of which was that she had to discover what had happened to her mother's plane.

She had to be strong.

She'd always believed it was her faith in God that would see her through. But with nitrogen bubbles coursing through her blood, hypothermia threatening to sink and drown her, and men who were trying to kill her, Sylvie struggled to trust God to see her through. How much could she trust Him? How much did she do on her own?

Right now she had never felt more alone. Had never had to draw on her own strength, or even on her faith in God, in this way before.

Like her dry suit, her faith and strength failed her.

Will couldn't leave without the woman. Neither could he stay with a man taking shots at him and his plane. He'd landed here because she'd been running in this direction. Now where was she?

In his Champ, he skipped across the water's surface, searching and praying. If he saw nothing, he would circle the island and come back to this spot, but he needed to draw the rifleman away from her. She could be hiding in the woods and afraid to run for the plane.

There!

The woman breached the water and waved, not twenty-five yards from him. If he hadn't been looking in the right direction at that exact moment, he might have missed her. Now to get her out of here without getting either of them killed. He slowed the plane, guided it close...closer...until he was as close as he could get without risking harm to her.

"You'll have to swim the rest of the way," he called. "Can you do that?"

The way she dipped below the water, that desperate look on her face, he wasn't sure she had any reserves left enough to swim all the way. But she was already swimming toward him even as the words left his mouth.

He stood on the pontoon and leaned out, encouraging her and at the same time glancing intermittently to the shore, watching for the shooter. They had to hurry.

"Come on, you can make it."

Determination flooded her features as she inched forward. Will reached for her at the same moment she grabbed on to the pontoon. She rested her head against it, catching her breath. Intelligent hazel eyes stared up, measuring him, her bluish lips quivering.

He thrust his hand out. "We need to get out of here."

She grabbed his hand and held his gaze. "Thank you."

Rifle fire exploded in the distance. They both instinctively ducked, but other than the plane itself, there was no cover.

"Hurry." He assisted her up and into the plane, not missing that she was bleeding from a gash in her suit. She needed help in more ways than one.

When she was secured in the seat, he found a blanket and threw it over her, then quickly secured himself and headed away from land. Another chink let him know his plane had taken another hit.

A wonder the rifleman hadn't succeeded in killing them already. But depending on the damage to the plane, the outcome remained to be seen. If he felt any trouble he could land them quickly enough, but he had to get them away from this place. He lifted off the water and glanced at her, noticing she visibly paled.

"You're not going to get sick on me, are you?"

Shivering, she shook her head. "I don't know. Maybe."

Well, which was it? But he wouldn't give her a hard time.

"I need to get my diving gear."

"You've got to be kidding me."

She stared at him, the gold flecks in her hazel eyes blazing. "Please. I appreciate your help, the risk to your life, everything you've done, but I might need to treat myself for decompression sickness."

"You're with me now. I'll get you to Juneau where they can treat you." Treating oneself was never a good idea.

"Can we just do a flyby to see if it's safe or not?"

It didn't sound as if she believed he would get her to Juneau. Will held back anything derogatory he might have said. "All right. Where is it?"

"I stashed it on the north side of the island where I'd been diving. There was a boat there last I saw, so that might mean trouble for us."

"I don't suppose now would be a good time for you to tell me what's going on."

"I would if I could. I don't know exactly. I was scuba diving when another diver appeared and tried to kill me. I escaped and swam to the surface, but my boat was missing. I swam to the island and barely made it out of the water and stowed my gear when I saw the man with the rifle. I'd been running from him, well, until you came along."

"And you believed you could trust me?" Now that almost had him grinning.

"When he shot at you, I knew you were here to help."

Will banked to the right, flying around the island to the north, hoping the boat she'd mentioned would be long gone. He looked her over. She'd tugged the hood of her dry suit off and worked the blanket over her medium-length hair to dry it. He wouldn't say she was pretty, in so many words, but she definitely had a presence about her that he might find compelling if he was looking to be compelled.

"There's the boat. We might have a chance." Will kept his disappointment in check. "But we need to make this quick. Where's your gear?"

She pointed. "Over there along the shoreline in the trees. See that big, funny-looking boulder?"

"And you're sure this is a good idea?"

"No."

Just what he wanted to hear. "I like an honest woman."

Will brought the plane down on the water and eased

up against a sandbar. He pulled out his weapon. "You stay put. Tell me where exactly, and I'll find it."

Her eyes grew wide. "No, you don't have to risk your life for me."

A little late for that, but he didn't say as much. Without another word he hopped from his plane. "Where?"

She pointed. "Just there, by that larger boulder."

The rifleman was well on the other side of the island, but Will didn't know who else he might have to contend with. Wary of his surroundings, weapon at the ready, he crept forward until he spotted her diving gear— double tanks. He hated the sight of them. Diving had killed his father. He grabbed the tanks but couldn't get a grip on the fins as well as hold his weapon in case he needed to use it.

She appeared next to him and snatched up the rest. Regulator, mask, snorkel, fins and buoyancy vest. "It's all important."

Carrying her dive equipment, they hurried back to the plane. Will noticed the boat heading their way. "We're out of time."

He lugged the tanks into the back as she tossed in the rest of her gear. Then he started the plane, speeding away on the water as he waited for her to secure herself in the seat.

Once they were airborne again and flying safely away from the boat and the island, Will glanced over at her.

Eyes closed, she pressed her head against the seat. "You said you're taking me to Juneau, right?"

"Unless you have a better idea."

"As long as they have a hyperbaric chamber." She opened her eyes, but squeezed the armrest.

"I'm flying low enough, the pressure shouldn't cause you more DCS problems." She didn't seem to find that comforting.

The plane hit turbulence. Will had long ago learned to ride the waves in the air—better to flow with them than to fight them. But his passenger's face went a shade whiter. These flights were rough on most others who weren't accustomed.

He had to get her mind off it. "What's your name?"

"Sylvie... Sylvie Masters." She gripped the armrest so hard, he thought she might break it.

She didn't ask for his name in return, but it was that moment when he should give it. Billy Pierson was the name everyone called him. Will had never much liked the name Billy as a kid, and wasn't sure why he continued to put up with it as an adult. With his father gone, changing it seemed almost disrespectful. But now his mother, who had called him Will, was gone, too. Maybe it was time he changed things out of respect for her.

Even though Sylvie didn't ask, Will told her anyway. "You can call me Will. I'm Will Pierson."

And with the pronouncement he felt the slightest hitch in his plane, a very unfamiliar sensation that had nothing at all to do with turbulence.

THREE

"Will. I like that name." She squeezed her eyes shut again, forcing her mind on anything but the bouncing plane. She was powerless against the jarring movement that barraged her with images of a rodeo cowboy riding a disgruntled bull. Her stomach roiling, she prayed she'd last more than the required eight seconds before being thrown.

Tossing a quick glance at Will, she hoped he hadn't noticed her distress, though it was not likely he would have missed it. His black hair was neatly trimmed beneath his Mountain Cove Air ball cap. It looked as if he was trying to grow a beard, or he hadn't shaved in a few days. Though he looked barely thirty—late twenties even—he had an edge to him, an aura of experience about him that made him seem older. Despite his jacket, she could tell he was strong and fit.

"If you hadn't shown up when you did, I don't know what I would have done. My options had run out. But in helping me, you might have gotten yourself wrapped up in my troubles."

"And what are your troubles?"

"You know as much as I do. I don't know why someone would want to kill me." Sylvie wished she hadn't said the words out loud. They disturbed her. She quickly changed the subject. Riding in the death trap of a plane was enough to handle at the moment. "Where're you from, Will?"

"Mountain Cove."

Sylvie couldn't help the shiver that ran across her shoulders. Her mother would have snarled at the mention of Mountain Cove. From all she'd told Sylvie, Mountain Cove was nothing but a bunch of backwater, back-stabbing gossipers. Her mother had reason enough to feel that way, Sylvie supposed, considering she'd had a secret affair with an already married pillar of the community and the man had ended his relationship with her. Pregnant, Sylvie's mother had been ashamed and fled Mountain Cove.

Sylvie kept to herself the fact that her father was from Mountain Cove. She'd never met him, though that would be impossible now that he was deceased. But her half siblings lived there, too. A surreal desperation flooded her—she wanted to meet the Warren siblings—her half siblings. See what they were made of. Come to her own conclusions about them, and what her real father was like and the people of Mountain Cove.

Despite all Sylvie's mother's negative talk about the town, she'd been on her way back to Mountain Cove for reasons unknown to Sylvie when she'd taken that last, fatal flight. But Sylvie didn't want to share any of this with Will. She didn't know a thing about him except that he'd saved her today.

The plane lurched to the right and Sylvie's stomach went with it. She released a telling groan.

"It gets rough through here. Sorry."

"So far it's been a walk in the meadow." Sylvie regretted her sarcasm. Will didn't deserve it.

But he laughed. He had a sense of humor, which was more than Sylvie could say for herself. Somehow the thick timbre of his mirth relaxed her.

"You never did say where you're from, by the way."

No, she hadn't. He hadn't asked, but normal conversation would have required she reciprocate when he'd told her he was from Mountain Cove.

"The Seattle area. I teach scuba diving for commercial divers and I volunteer for search-and-rescue dive operations."

The man next to her shifted in his seat and seemed uneasy. "My dad died in a diving accident. I haven't gone diving since."

"I'm sorry to hear that. My mother died in a plane crash." She regretted her tone. She hadn't meant it to sound as though she was in a competition.

The plane jerked with his reaction, subtle though it was. "Well, we have something in common, after all. My mother died in a plane crash, too."

Oh, why had she revealed so much? She wasn't sure what more she should tell him, if anything. He didn't deserve to get mixed up in her problems. But what if he already was? Had the men who tried to kill her today paid attention to Will and his plane? Would they track him down and exact some sort of killing revenge?

She should have realized this from the beginning. The attack on her today must have to do with her mother's plane crash. She was close to finding the crash and someone didn't want her there. What else could it be? Or was she exhibiting the crazy imagination of someone suffering through mild hypothermia and the bends all at the same time?

A snippet of her mother's voice mail raced across her mind.

I'm flying to Mountain Cove on a bush plane. I know what you're thinking, but I'll tell you more when I get there. It's Damon... Oh... I've gotta go...

A rattling din—something entirely new—rose above the whir of the propellers, and a tremor joined the rattle. Was this normal? She squeezed the armrests again because there wasn't anything else to grab. Sylvie's warnings to her mother about flying came rushing back, swirling with images of her mother. Her relationship with Sylvie's stepfather, Damon Masters, and the endless arguments.

Secrets.

Was her life flashing before her eyes like she'd so often heard would happen in the last few moments of life?

"What's happening?"

When Will didn't answer, she risked opening her eyes. His features were tight.

Okay, well, that doesn't look good. "If I survive this, I'm never flying again. I wouldn't be on this plane now if I had any other choice. No offense."

"None taken." His voice had an edge to it. "You miss out on a lot if you don't fly. You'll never see the world like this, see the wonders of Alaska, if you don't get in the air and soar with the eagles."

"Are you saying this is normal?" Her teeth clattered along with the plane.

"You just have to roll with it if you can. But if it makes you feel any better, I know what I'm doing."

Then the plane lurched to the left, and a sound like

the crack of thunder rocked the plane, vibrated through her core. "Will, I can't die today. I have to find my mother's plane!"

Her words held some kind of meaning for him personally, but he couldn't figure it out when their survival was on the line, so he tucked them inside his mind to pick apart later. He'd just reassured her he was a good pilot. He needed to live up to his word.

"You've been honest with me to a point, so I'll be honest with you. I think the rifleman might have done some damage to the plane. It's taken time to work its way through, and now we're feeling the pain of it."

"What are you saying?"

"I'm saying I'm a good pilot—a great pilot—but it never hurts to say your prayers. Get your affairs in order with God."

"Are you kidding me?"

"I wouldn't kid you about something so serious." He hated to scare her, but neither could he hide the gravity of the situation.

As he struggled to bring the vibrating plane in, to find a body of water on which to land, he thought back to his mother. Was this how she'd felt when her plane was going down? She'd been a great pilot, too. The best. And yet his mother's plane was missing. It had to have crashed somewhere. What had Sylvie said about needing to find her mother's plane? He couldn't think about that now—he had to focus on keeping them alive.

A friend lived within hiking distance of the strip of water he aimed for. Even if they landed safely, Sylvie wouldn't survive without some place warm to wait until help arrived.

The plane kicked, a rumble spilling through the fuselage. His gut tensed.

Though he struggled to grip the vibrating yoke, he reached over and pressed his hand over Sylvie's white knuckles that squeezed the armrest. Surprising him, she released her grip and held his hand, strong and tight. Maybe it had nothing at all to do with reality but more to do with looking death straight in the eyes, but Will had a sense of connection with Sylvie Masters—a complete stranger—which made no sense.

God, please let me save Sylvie. Save the day. Like her, I want to find my mother's plane. Find the answers. Then he understood what his mind could not comprehend earlier.

God had to have brought them together for this same purpose. They couldn't die today.

"We're going to be okay, Sylvie. Just keep praying."

Her reply came out in an indistinguishable murmur. Indistinguishable but understandable, all the same. She fought to hold herself together. He couldn't blame her. He didn't want to release her hand, finding a comfort in her grip that he hadn't known he needed, but he pulled away and gripped the yoke.

"There, see the water? That's all I need for a smooth landing." He thought of his mother again. That was all she would have needed, too. He'd long begun to suspect her plane hadn't crashed where they could find debris, but had gone down and sunk to the bottom of the ocean, a channel somewhere, just waiting to be discovered like a shipwreck full of treasure.

The thought sickened him. His stomach pitched with the plane. Sylvie hunched over her knees, covered her head as if she was prepared to crash. As if her efforts would save her.

Will couldn't be sure they would land on the water or that he could keep his word. Rain pelted the windshield, and as comfortable with flying as any bush pilot could be, he had to admit—but only to himself—this had been the ride of his life.

He piloted the plane forward and tried again to radio for help, but they were still in no-man's-land.

"Sylvie?"

She mumbled. Groaned. Kept her head down.

"Promise me something."

Another groan.

"Promise me you *will* fly again."

"Are you crazy?"

At least he'd gotten a coherent response from her. "Promise me."

"You mean if we survive?"

"Yes. I mean if I land this broken hull of a plane and we climb out of it in one piece."

"If I say yes will you try harder to land?"

The crack in her desperate voice sent him tumbling.

"Sylvie, I couldn't try any harder, but I thought I'd take the opportunity to extract a promise from you. I wouldn't want you to miss out on seeing the world the way I see it."

Sylvie stared at him, wide-eyed. "Why would you care how I see the world?"

Will couldn't say why it was important to him, but in that instant, facing a one-of-a-kind death, he knew it was. He opened his mouth to reply but the plane shuddered and plummeted. Water swallowed them, then everything went black.

FOUR

Water rushed into the plane that had hit too hard. Sylvie fought the panic. Sucked in air hard and fast. Must. Slow. Breathing. Hyperventilating would do her no good. Passing out wasn't an option. One of them had to get the two of them out.

With Will unconscious that would leave Sylvie.

Forget what she'd already been through. Survive. She had to survive—to reach down and find strength she didn't know she had.

Water poured in.

The plane was sinking.

Sinking?

Sylvie had always thought floatplanes were, well, supposed to float. But then she remembered Jacques Cousteau's son, also a diver, who died in a floatplane that crashed and sank.

Surely the pontoons would prevent it from completely submerging. Wasn't that the whole purpose of pontoons on a floatplane? But that didn't mean that Will wouldn't drown in the meantime.

A small gash in his forehead bled. She unbuckled the

strap, bracing herself for the rush forward into water that had quickly covered the controls.

Sylvie pressed a finger against Will's neck, confirming he was still alive. She couldn't accept anything less. Then she worked to unbuckle him from the shoulder harness, but it wouldn't budge.

"Come on!" she yelled at the buckle.

What she wouldn't give for her diver's knife. It had to be in here somewhere. They were both fortunate her tanks hadn't flown forward and cracked their heads during the impact.

"Will, come on, you need to wake up."

The plane creaked and groaned. It would pitch completely over and upside down soon, and then Will's head would be fully under water. They would both be. Sylvie searched his pockets.

There.

She found a pocketknife.

But before she set him free, she opened his door, left it hanging forward before the water pressure could seal it shut. More water rushed in at the bottom.

She was running out of time.

Quickly she sawed through his shoulder strap. Though she prepared to catch Will, his dead weight fell forward on her and smashed her against the dashboard, the yoke gouging into her back. The blow knocked the air from her lungs. She worked to push his head above the waterline.

Now to get him out. They were going to make it. She could do this. Sylvie slipped by him in the small space then tugged him out into the water. She'd swim him to shore, keeping his head high. This was lifeguard 101, and was actually much easier to do with an unconscious victim than one who was awake and struggling.

With regret, she left her diving equipment in the plane to save Will. She wouldn't think ahead, wouldn't concern herself with what to do, until she made it to shore. She positioned him on his back and hooked her arms under his armpits. On her back, she swam them to shore. She tried to keep her thoughts from what she might face—the immediate danger of exposure to the elements—and instead focused on what she could do. After all, two men had tried to kill her, and this seemed small in comparison.

She could swim.

Had been born with a natural affinity for water.

You're in your element, Sylvie.

Just breathe. Swim. Save Will.

Regardless of her attempts at self-assurance, feeble though they were, fear twisted inside, corded in the sinews of her muscles. She hadn't expected things to turn this way. Hadn't expected to face death twice in one day.

Bad enough someone had tried to kill her. Worse, she'd almost died in a plane crash like her mother. Though she'd admit that Will's plane—and Will himself—had saved her the first part of the day. And Will would be sick about the loss once he woke up.

He *would* wake up.

He had to wake up.

Her back scraped across pebbles and sand and rocks. Ignoring the pain, she dragged Will the rest of the way onto a small strip of sand. Sylvie examined his head then the rest of him. She could see no other injury besides the gash in his head that was no longer bleeding so profusely. Hopefully, it would stop soon. She had nothing with which to staunch the flow.

She could swim back and get a first-aid kit from the plane before it sank. Or her scuba equipment! But her body was too cold. It wouldn't be safe. She might not make it back.

She held his face in her hands. "Will, can you hear me?"

He'd lost his ball cap in the melee, and his hair was thicker than she'd initially thought. He had a jutting chin on a nice strong jaw. She felt strange holding his face, touching him like this. It seemed entirely too intimate with someone who was practically a stranger, but this was a matter of life and death. She didn't think he would care. She wished he would open his eyes—those warm brown eyes. Though she hadn't appreciated his questions or his humor at first, the warmth in his tone had comforted her when she'd needed it.

"Will," she whispered. "If you'll wake up, I might just agree to fly again."

But Will didn't respond. The cold water hadn't shocked him awake like she would have expected. It had shocked her system, though, and she was shivering even now. She released his face, hating that his color wasn't good. Looking at the thick temperate rain forest behind her and across the water on the other side, she studied the mountains peaking above the treetops in the distance.

She knew enough about the geography to believe they were somewhere south, way south of Juneau. Far enough that it might as well have been a thousand miles. Sylvie dropped to where the water lapped and pressed her head into her knees.

Just what was she supposed to do now?

* * *

Cold prickles stung his face. Shivering, Will opened his eyes to raindrops bombarding him, along with what felt like an anvil pounding his temples.

Where am I?

His mind raced, competing with his pulse as he pushed up and caught sight of the woman sitting next to him, face pressed against her knees. Guilt tackled him. Though his mind was fuzzy, he somehow knew he'd failed her.

"Sylvie." He reached over and pressed his hand against her arm. "Are you okay?"

Lifting her head, she turned to face him, her hazel eyes drawing him in. "Will, I'm so glad... I thought you were..."

Will couldn't understand why she was still here. She was going to die if she didn't get someplace warm. He would, too, for that matter. They'd both been soaked to the bone, and right now the temperature wasn't much different on the ground than in the water. It was his fault she was here now. Somehow it was his fault. But his mind still struggled to understand.

Think, Will, think.

Then the all-too-fresh memories rolled over him. "How long have I been out?"

She lifted her shoulders as if called to action. "Not that long. The plane..." Sylvie looked out to the water.

Will followed her gaze. He stood, taking it all in. He'd nearly gotten them both killed. Something had gone wrong—something partly out of his hands, out of his control. But he should have improvised or adjusted. Why was that part still such a blur? He raked his arm across his eyes and forehead. It came away smeared with blood.

"You're okay," she said. "The bleeding stopped."

He drew her to her feet while he stared at his plane, completely flipped nose down and sinking. "I've never personally seen that happen."

Nor had he experienced anything like it. That he'd lost a plane today, to add to the loss of his mother's plane, pressed against nerve centers he hadn't known he possessed. But that was nothing compared to losing his mother.

Still, none of these thoughts would help Sylvie. Getting her someplace warm and safe was his priority. And knowing he had a mission, someone to help, would keep his head in the game, despite his losses.

"How did I get here?" He looked back at her, grateful the rain had eased up. "You pulled me out and swam me to safety?"

She nodded, rubbed her arms.

"Thank you."

"I didn't know where to go after that, what to do. Seemed like I was back where I started, only with an injured man this time. But at least no one is trying to find and kill me at the moment."

As far as you know. But he didn't voice his thoughts.

Will hoped that would remain the case for a long while. Forever would be nice. He grabbed her hand and squeezed. "It's going to be okay, Sylvie. We're going to be okay."

Those words reminded him of something else, but he couldn't quite remember what. Something hovered at the edge of his mind. Something about today that con-

nected him to Sylvie. He hoped he'd remember while
it still mattered.

A smile softened her grim features. He hadn't thought
her pretty at first, but now he changed his mind. Her
smile brightened her eyes and emphasized appealing
dimples against soft, smooth skin. Something else thrived
behind her determined gaze that drew him to her.

Her shiver snapped his focus back to where it should
be.

"I have a friend who lives not too far. I'm sure he
saw us go down—I'm surprised he hasn't already shown
up." That was only partially true. He'd said the man was
a friend, but in fact, he was only a client and a recluse
who liked his privacy. Will had no idea what reaction
they would get when they showed up. Will had never
actually been invited to the cabin, but knew from flying over where it was relative to the beach.

"Are you okay to walk?"

"Yes, lead the way." She hugged herself.

"Good. Shouldn't take long." He trudged ahead of
her.

Will wished he could hold her close to share some
body heat, but that would be awkward. He didn't think
they were that desperate yet. Yes, Sylvie had taken a
beating today. With her ripped suit, circles under her
eyes, bluish skin and lips, anyone could look at her and
see how badly she'd been hurt. But in her eyes, those
hazel eyes, Will saw her unbridled determination and
knew she wouldn't accept his help.

What man could help but admire her?

They neared the tree line and he followed the brook
that would eventually lead them to the off-grid cabin
where John Snake lived. Snake—he liked the nick-

name to keep out the riffraff—usually met Will near the beach for his packages, but that was when he knew to expect Will.

He turned to check on Sylvie, but she was farther behind than he'd thought. Frowning, he made his way back. She was strong, but she'd been through a lot both before and after he'd come on the scene in his float-plane.

"Hey, you doing okay?"

Seeing her purse her lips, he got the sense she wanted to smile, but couldn't. "How much farther?"

Will hated to tell her it was still a couple more miles, and the terrain wasn't getting any easier. Add to that, the rain was icy cold and coming down harder.

He didn't like the glazed look in her eyes. "A mile, maybe."

She dropped to a log and hung her head. "Okay. I can do that. I just… I think I might have sprained my ankle. These diving boots are no good in this type of terrain."

He frowned. "No kidding."

"Give me a minute to rest."

Was she serious? Will wouldn't expect her to walk if she was injured. In fact, he shouldn't have let her walk to the cabin even before finding out about her ankle. What with hypothermia setting in and she hinting at having decompression sickness, she was in a world of hurt, but he didn't want to step on her strong and capable toes, so he hadn't offered any help.

Until now. There wasn't time to rest. They had to get out of the weather.

He scraped his arms under her knees and around her back and lifted her.

"What are you doing?" Alarm jumped from her gaze and her voice.

Will settled her against him until she felt right. She was lean and solid, as divers tended to be, but light enough he could manage the distance. "Don't take offense, Sylvie. I need to get you out of this weather."

Her gaze softened. "Thank you. I didn't mean for you to have to do this."

"I figure I owe you. After all, you pulled me from a sinking plane and swam me to shore. Saved my life. So it's my turn to carry you." There. Hopefully, he hadn't offended her strong and capable woman sensibilities.

Sylvie didn't argue and instead rested her head against his shoulder. That ignited familiar feelings inside. Protective feelings. He'd forgotten he could feel that way and instantly remembered why he hadn't wanted to. A year ago he'd given it all to Michelle and she'd made a fool of him, practically leading him around town by the proverbial ring in his nose until she'd dumped him. In the end she couldn't take the fact Will was a bush pilot. He was gone all the time and he wasn't there to do her bidding or entertain her. She'd claimed she was afraid he would die out there in the bush and she'd be left alone. It was her or flying. He'd had a choice to make.

So he'd come back early, canceled a job and was almost ready to give it all up for her—against his mother's strong advice, of course—when he found Michelle with someone else.

Everyone had seen the fool that Will had been except for Will until it was too late.

He wouldn't allow that to happen again. But this situation had nothing to do with that one.

Two different women.

Two different scenarios.

If Sylvie had any hint of his thoughts she'd be out of his arms in a second, and that would do neither of them any good. Will had to get his mind off Sylvie's proximity. He tried to focus on the steps he took rather than the warmth of Sylvie's body against his.

If he could get her talking about what happened today, maybe it would distract him and they could find some answers to boot.

"Tell me about those men, Sylvie. Why did they try to kill you?"

"I already told you I don't know anything."

Was she telling the truth? "So this was just random, then? Two men were there, and you were at the wrong place at the wrong time? What could you have stumbled on? I can't imagine they were out there minding their own business and decided to kill whoever showed up for no reason."

Had she stumbled on something and was hiding that fact? There had to be much more to this story. That something gnawed at his mind again, just out of his reach. A cup of warm coffee and some rest might ease the ache in his head and set him thinking clearly again.

She released a sigh that tickled his neck. "Obviously I have a lot to figure out, but I can't think a straight thought."

"Right. You need food and warmth and sleep." Just like he did. If only he could find that cabin. He hoped he didn't run into those men after Sylvie. But they couldn't have followed him. He'd take comfort in that. Then again, letting down his guard could be a mistake neither of them could afford.

Too many unknowns made him edgier by the second.

As the cold rain came down harder, tumbling through the canopy of spruce and hemlock, Will focused on stepping his way over slick boulders and freezing ground, careful to avoid slipping, especially with his burden. Though Sylvie was small, carrying her the distance began to weigh on him. His arms ached, challenging his confidence. He should have come across Snake's cabin by now. If he wasn't going to find the cabin, then they needed to make shelter while there was still enough light.

The rain eased to a fine mist, blunted by the forest canopy.

He stopped, thinking about putting her down so he could build a fire.

"Will." Her warm breath caressed his cheek. "Through the woods..."

Will's pulse jumped. The cabin? He peered through the trees, eyes following where she gestured. An elk. Disappointment jabbed through him that it wasn't the cabin. How could he tell her the disheartening news that he didn't know where he was going, after all? He set her down, steadying her to sit on a fallen log, and drew in a breath to tell her the bad news. Before he could say the words, the fog in his mind lifted, and he saw clearly what he couldn't understand before.

Sylvie had been looking for her mother's missing plane—the same as him.

His next words took a different tack altogether.

"Tell me about the plane you were looking for." Ever since she mentioned her mother's plane, Will suspected they were both on the same search. His mother's plane was the only one that had gone missing in the area in more than a year, and there had been one passenger. A woman. Sylvie's mother—he was sure of it. And from the look on her face, she was making the connection, too.

"You're a bush pilot. Mountain Cove Air. That's your company?"

He nodded. "My mother was flying a surprise package back to Mountain Cove two months ago when her plane went missing. I've been searching for her ever since. I think we've both been looking for the same plane." How could it have flown so far off the intended path that search parties—Alaska Air National Guard, Alaska State Troopers, Alaska Fire Service, Coast Guard, Fish and Wildlife Guard, the list went on—hadn't found them? Then again, they had thousands of square miles of islands, water and mountains to search even on the flight path she should have taken. Not counting where she might have detoured.

That was it, then. She'd taken a detour and Will suddenly knew. Why hadn't he thought of that before? She'd kept a postcard his father had sent her years before of a beautiful waterfall. What if his mother had been showing Sylvie's mother the sights, including her favorite?

Will remembered the postcard because of the scripture quote written on it. "But they that wait upon the Lord shall renew their strength; they shall mount up with wings as eagles; they shall run, and not be weary; and they shall walk, and not faint." Isaiah 40:31

From the moment he'd seen the postcard and read the verse, Will had always pictured himself as an eagle when he flew. Seeing life from above, the big picture of things, must be how God saw things.

Could the plane be there?

Sylvie rubbed her arms. "Oh, Will."

"Do you know anything about a surprise package?" he asked. "I keep wondering if…" He couldn't bring himself to say the worst. He didn't want to believe his mother had delivered a surprise that turned out to be an actual explosive device. The idea was too far-fetched.

"I think the surprise was my mother. She lived in Mountain Cove years ago. She left after she had an affair with a married man. It was a bad breakup. And then she found out she was pregnant. She had to leave."

Will hated where this was going. Hated it for Sylvie. "Was she pregnant with you?"

"Yes." She hesitated then added, "My mother's name was Regina Hemphill. My father was Scott Warren. I have half brothers and one half sister. Maybe you know them."

"I do." He released a heavy sigh. "That is *one* surprise package. But you're an even bigger surprise."

"Yeah, a surprise nobody wants to hear about. Or at least, that's what my mother told me as gently as she could when she explained why I shouldn't try to contact my father or half siblings. I guess she didn't want to see me get my expectations up and get hurt. I can't be sure she even told him about me. When I finally worked up the nerve to face him on my own, I couldn't because he had died." She shivered, either from the memory or from the chill in the air.

Will was reminded that he needed to find shelter. They could search for a cave, but what if they didn't find one in time? He needed to build at least a rudimentary cover. A debris hut would be quick and easy and keep them warm. He'd prefer a bough structure to reflect the warmth of a fire. The problem was a rainforest was much too wet, and the chances he could start a fire were close to zero.

God, please, we need Snake's cabin.

"It's not fair," she whispered. "And I have half siblings who may not even know I'm alive. I can't tell you how often I've thought of them, wanted to meet them."

Strange to think her mother, given the circumstances of her having to leave Mountain Cove, would have told Sylvie about her half siblings. Or had she done her own research? But she wasn't finished talking and he wouldn't interrupt. Instead, he began creating a mound from the forest floor.

"On the other side of that, they could resent me for the reminder that their father betrayed his marriage vows with my mother. They could hate me. So it's almost better if I never meet them. Then I can stick with believing they'd want to meet me, but don't know if I exist or how to find me if I did." Sylvie groaned. "I can't believe I'm telling you all this. You didn't exactly ask for the whole shebang."

"I know the Warren siblings would love to meet you." He knew the siblings were aware of their father's affair, and knew they'd tried to find out if they had a brother or sister out there. These were conversations he couldn't help but overhear when piloting the Warrens to Juneau or sometimes even delivering them to a SAR—search and rescue—command center. They trusted Will. But in all of this, what he'd really like to know was if his mother had known where Regina had gone all along, but said nothing. "I'll help you make that happen."

"No, please, no. I'm not sure I'm ready to face them. I'm torn about it. I need time to think it through. I want

it to be on my terms. Please don't ever tell them. I'll be
the one if it happens."

"Okay, then." If Will's mother had kept Regina's secret, he thought he could feel some of what she might
have felt when someone extracted a promise like that.

Still, it would be a hard promise to keep, depending
on how all of this unfolded. From what had happened
so far, this seemed to be shaping up into quite an adventure that Will could tell his grandchildren about one
day. But he couldn't think of it as an adventure until it
was over and they survived. Grandchildren? He'd never
get married so children were out of the question.

Will needed to excavate a hole in the debris, and
then he and Sylvie would have to crawl into the pile,
supported by loose branches, and hope to keep warm.
Tomorrow he could build something better, if it came
to that.

She tilted her head. "I thought you were making a
fire."

"A fire? It's too wet."

"Oh, I guess you're right. I should be helping you."
Sylvie stood then fell back to the log.

"You're injured. No need to help." Will took a short
break and sat next to Sylvie on the log, hoping his body
heat would warm her, wishing his headache would sub-
side.

"I know it's hard to understand how I can ask you
to keep my secret. Mom made it sound like the whole
town of Mountain Cove gossiped about her. Practically
ran her out of town. That's why I need to work up my
nerve before approaching the Warrens."

"You? You've got nerves of steel." Will inserted some

humor into this too-serious conversation to cover his own growing anxiety about their chances of survival.

"Nerves of steel don't matter. Under the right circumstances even something as benign as salt can turn corrosive and erode steel." Sylvie shifted next to him. "Despite her feelings about the town, she was on her way back to Mountain Cove. I guess I'll never understand why, but I wanted to find her plane. I want to know what happened."

"You and me both, Sylvie. You and me both." Will waited for Sylvie to go on, one question burning in his mind. When she didn't continue, he asked, "Did you find what you were looking for? Did you find the plane?"

Sylvie opened her mouth to speak.

A twig snapped from the shadows. Will sprang from the log to face the threat. He stood in front of Sylvie to protect her and reached for his weapon, but came up empty-handed. He'd forgotten that he didn't have it. It was submerged with his plane.

Wearing a hood, a man emerged from the trees. Friend or foe?

"Snake?" Will squinted, studying the intruder.

The man stepped forward and tugged back his hood. "What are you doing here?"

FIVE

What kind of name is that?

Will glanced over his shoulder at Sylvie. She stood from the log, easing onto her good foot and using Will's back for support. She wanted to be standing in case they needed to make a run for it.

"Sorry for the unannounced visit, Snake. You know I'd never intrude if it wasn't an emergency. But I had some plane trouble. A hard landing and Sylvie and I... we've had a brush with death or two today."

The man's expression darkened as he studied both Sylvie and Will. It seemed that he had issues with trust. Clearly he lived a reclusive life away from civilization. Away from the prying eyes of the law. She wouldn't second-guess his reasons. This wasn't her world.

"Come on, then." He turned and disappeared into the trees.

Will lifted her back in his arms and followed. "Only a little longer, Sylvie. You hanging in there? Doing okay?"

"I'm good, thanks to you."

"You'll be thanking Snake before too long. He's the one with the cabin and a warm fire. I bet he'll have a big pot of game stewing, too. That's what I'd do in this weather if I were him."

Sylvie's mouth watered at the mention of food. She could already imagine the warm fire and wanted nothing more than to sleep in a soft bed, covers piled high. Safe, sound and secure. She sighed at the thought. Was that asking too much?

But she had to remain vigilant. This wasn't over yet. She couldn't rest until it was. And Will deserved an answer to his question. "No. I didn't find the plane. I thought I saw something, though. The glint of what could have been part of a plane. That's when I was attacked."

Lines pressed between his brows.

"There's something else," she whispered. "I'm grateful for your help and for Snake's, but you know I need to get out of here. I need a decompression chamber. And I don't want to put anyone else in danger."

There, she'd said the words that had been crawling over her ever since Will had made an appearance today and put himself between her and the men trying to kill her.

"One thing at a time," he said. "Snake has a radio. While I was in the air trying to figure out how to rescue you, I tried to radio for help a few times, but no one connected on the other end." He glanced at her, his strong, scruffy jaw and warm brows much too close. "I'll make the call for help first thing. Only Snake isn't going to like it."

"Why not?" But she thought she already knew.

"He lives off-grid. Doesn't want anyone to know he's here. Doesn't want to draw attention to his castle in the glen. Once people know about his castle, he might be overrun with marauders."

"Out here? Nah, I doubt it." Sylvie couldn't help but grin at his medieval references. He was definitely chivalrous, a real knight in shining armor, now that she thought about it. With his strong arms holding her, carrying her over and through the terrain—not an easy task in places—and keeping her pressed against his warm, muscular form, she couldn't think straight.

She had to get her mind on something else. She was strong and independent, and didn't like that being near him turned her soft and compliant. Made her needy. She couldn't afford to be like her mother when it came to men, and get hurt in the worst of ways. With all that had happened today, she feared her suspicions that her mother had been murdered were confirmed, and she'd almost blurted it all out to Will. She wasn't ready to tell him her darkest of secrets yet. Not until she was absolutely certain of it. She didn't want to think about it now, didn't want to face the truth of what that would mean. So she turned her thoughts back to Will and Snake.

"But *you* know where he lives."

"That, I do. He needs someone he can trust to bring him supplies *and* keep his existence a secret."

"Are you telling me the Alaska State Troopers or the Coast Guard or some other entity doesn't know he's here?"

"Maybe they do, maybe they don't. The point is that he is off the grid and off the radar. Or at least, he was."

"And now you've blown his trust."

"He invited us to follow him, didn't he?"

"Doesn't mean he'll let you use his radio."

"That remains to be seen."

Sylvie wasn't sure she liked Will's answer. Was he going to use the radio or not? And if not, how did they get out of here? The need to get them out of his sanctuary should be reason enough for Snake to let them call for help.

Sylvie could barely make out the man's silhouette ahead of them since he made better time, crept stealthily through the forest much faster than Will, who carried Sylvie. Once again, she found the need to distract herself from Will's sturdy body, and the great care and attention he took to making the ride as smooth as possible despite the slick, sodden boulders and fallen trunks and debris he had to step over and around.

Finally, Will stood at the open door of Snake's log cabin and then carried Sylvie over the threshold.

"You can set her down over there." Snake referred to her as if she were a box of supplies and gestured to a long sofa near the woodstove.

Will was right. The man had something going on the stove, and the aroma stirred her hunger. After Will gently settled her on the sofa—worn out but more plush than she would have expected—Snake appeared by Will's side with a first-aid kit.

"Thanks." Will took the kit. "She needs dry clothes, too. Got any extras? I'll make sure to reimburse you."

"No need for that." Snake nodded and disappeared through a door off the main room.

"I agree," she said. "There's no need for you to reimburse Snake for any dry clothes he offers me. I'm perfectly capable of doing that myself."

At Will's surprised glance, she added, "And I'm perfectly capable of being grateful." She offered a smile of her own. "Thank you, Will, for your thoughtfulness.

For carrying me through the woods. I'm sorry you had to do that. Besides, you need them, too."

"What do I need?" Will crouched near her ankle and examined it.

"Dry clothes."

"I'll manage. And you're welcome, by the way. All in a day's work."

Yeah, right. When he touched her ankle, she winced.

"It's not so bad," he said, "And probably the least of your worries. Am I right?"

"You know you are."

He shot her a grin that tugged at her insides. She was losing it. Cold and hungry and injured and...well...that made her vulnerable. Sylvie wouldn't read anything into his grin. She couldn't afford to get sidetracked.

"I'll wrap this after you change out of the dry suit." Will stood when Snake appeared and held out a couple of large flannel shirts and some jeans.

"These do?"

Will cocked a brow at Sylvie, humor flickering in his gaze.

"It'll have to. Thank you, Snake." Saying his name felt awkward on her lips.

Will slung the extra clothes over his shoulder. "Thanks, Snake."

Sylvie hated to ask, hated to need help, but worse than that, she hated to limp across the floor. No, falling on her face would be worse. She had some vertigo. Not good. She hoped she only had a mild case of DCS. She'd never before gotten the bends. The dive hadn't been that deep, and she'd descended at the appropriate rate. But her ascending straight to the surface without any stops had been all it took to throw her body chemistry into turmoil. The cold water and exertion from fighting off a killer hadn't done her any favors.

The next few hours would be telling, especially if she didn't get help. But first things first. Right now she simply needed to make it to that room for some privacy. "Will, can you assist me to the room so I can change?"

"Sure thing. Um… Sylvie… I need to doctor that gash across your shoulder and back, too."

"You don't think that can wait?"

His grin from moments ago quickly faded. "No."

"I need to doctor your head," she said. Fair play.

"Snake has a mirror. I can take care of it."

But Sylvie couldn't reach her shoulder and back, even with a mirror, so that was that. She let the compassion and concern in Will's warm brown eyes calm her nerves. He was good in that way, even addicting if she wasn't careful.

"While you guys take care of business," Snake said, "I'll dish up the stew. Got strong coffee going, too. When you're ready, we'll eat."

"Sounds good." Will assisted Sylvie into what was obviously Snake's bedroom and set her on the bed. He frowned down at her.

All she wanted to do was lie down and sleep forever. This close to a bed, the warmth of the cabin and the aroma of the stew, she could sense the adrenaline crash coming.

Hold it together. Just a little longer.

"You okay to get out of that suit without any help?" His tone and the look in his eyes said his only concern was for her. He wasn't going to take advantage of her. She didn't trust easily, but he'd brought her this far. She wanted to trust him.

"Thanks, Will, but I can handle it."

"Good. Call me when you're ready."

"Okay." His words held tenderness that pricked her heart. She was definitely vulnerable. Somehow she had to get her guard back up. She'd been through too much already.

Her stepfather had been a wonderful father during her childhood. Someone she could trust, someone she had been proud to call *Dad*, until she'd become older and wiser. When she was a teenager, she discovered he was having an affair. The betrayal devastated Sylvie. She didn't know where to turn. She didn't want to hurt her mother, but finally shared his duplicity, only to learn that her mother already knew. How could her mother let him treat her like that? At first Sylvie thought her mother hadn't left because she loved him—which just proved how dangerous love could be. Sylvie built a wall around her heart that day. She could never trust anyone again. And from that moment on, she called him Damon.

But then, behind closed doors, she heard the arguments. Raised voices. Her mother crying. And then Sylvie began to suspect that her mother hadn't left Damon because she was afraid of him. Afraid to leave. Damon was a powerful man.

None of that mattered now, except to remind her to keep her guard up around Will. She needed to keep herself together until she was back home. Or at least in that decompression chamber.

Sitting on the edge of the bed, her ankle throbbing, every joint in her body aching badly enough to make her completely forget the open gash in her back, she drew in a breath and prepared to peel out of the dry suit and layers of clothing beneath. All she wanted was a hot shower, but she supposed the best she could get at an off-grid cabin was a sponge bath. She looked down to see the ripped, practically shredded suit. She hadn't wanted to look too closely. Seeing it now, a replay of the last few hours flashed through her mind, reel after reel.

All the way to her soul, Sylvie was torn and ripped like the dry suit she wore.

She pressed her face into her hands and let everything she'd held back come flooding out.

Will had changed quickly so he'd be ready to dress Sylvie's wound. Behind the door he could hear her quiet sobs. She'd been strong, held it together in front of him. He wasn't sure why the sound rocked through him, knocking against the hidden parts of his heart. He pressed a hand on the door as though he could comfort her. He didn't know this woman at all, but he didn't have to know her to feel the pain with her.

He let his hand drop. He wouldn't go rushing in. He wasn't a knight and she didn't want to be saved. If he knew anything at all about the woman shut away in the room, it was that she didn't want him to see her vulnerable. Sucking in a breath, he glanced up and caught Snake watching him from where he hovered over the fire, dishing up the stew that he cooked in a cast-iron pot hanging over the flames, old school.

Will had another situation he'd been avoiding. He needed to face off with Snake about using the radio to call for help. He knew the other man wouldn't be pleased. The harsh environment along with fifty-plus years had made the man hard and lean. He kept his long silver hair in a ponytail hanging down his back, and time spent away from civilization kept his expression harsh, especially when faced with having to make conversation. But he'd still saved them. Will would give him that. He hadn't been anything but helpful—so far.

Snake's bushy eyebrows creased together as he stood from the fire and held out a bowl. "You hungry?"

Will took the bowl, but set it on the table. "Thanks, but I'll wait for Sylvie."

"Suit yourself." Snake remained standing and wolfed up a few spoonfuls of his stew then paused, the spoon halfway to his mouth. "Something on your mind?"

Here comes the moment of truth. "I told you we had some trouble. That trouble includes men who tried to kill her, kill us. They shot at my plane. Caused some damage and we went down. I hope I haven't brought the trouble to your door."

Snake's eyes narrowed. He set his bowl on the home-crafted table and crossed his arms. "What do you need?"

"I need to use your comm to call for help."

Snake shook his head. "You're not bringing them here."

"You can see she's injured."

"Call them and make arrangements to meet them elsewhere. I'll help you get there."

Will scraped a hand over his face, exhaustion creeping into his bones. "She has the bends, and with her other injuries she needs treatment right away."

Snake's eyes lit up, surprising Will. "Why didn't you say something before?"

"Would it have made a difference?"

"I'm a diver. Got the equipment. Worst case, she could recompress in the water."

Will shook his head. "That *is* the worst case. It's too

risky. Better to wait for a hyperbaric chamber, which is why I need to use your radio."

"Well, you know the option is available. Why don't you tell her and let her make the decision? She isn't afraid of diving."

Had Will been that readable?

Snake disappeared through a door, reappearing a minute later to set his scuba equipment out in full view. Was that because he didn't trust Will to bring it up?

Will frowned.

"Make your call. Pick a meeting time and place. Early morning's best. Give us time to rest up and gather the gear we'll need."

"I can't ask for more than that."

Will hated to put it off that long, considering Sylvie needed assistance sooner rather than later, but Snake was right. If they were forced to travel to make contact, they couldn't do it in inclement weather in the middle of the night. He had to persuade Snake to shorten the distance they needed to travel.

"Just how far do you want us to go?"

"I don't want anyone coming within five miles of my cabin. That might sound harsh, Will, but let me remind you that if it was someone else I'd seen tromping through the woods, I wouldn't have shown my face. I wouldn't have offered an invitation into my home. I wouldn't even have opened my door."

"I know." Will was grateful to Snake. The man had chosen this lifestyle for reasons unknown to Will. He wouldn't pry.

"About those men who tried to kill you? You sure they didn't follow you here?"

"I don't see how they could have, but neither can I

be sure. I don't know who they are or why they tried to kill her." He had his suspicions. Some things were trying to fall into place, but mostly it was still a mystery.

"What do you know about her?"

"Nothing. I just happened to be flying overhead in time to see her running for her life." Will struggled with whether or not to share the full of it with Snake, considering he didn't particularly seem the kind of person who would want to know the details about others' lives, nor would he reciprocate. Best to keep things simple and not share that Will and Sylvie had both lost their mothers on the same MIA airplane. For now.

From Snake's expression, Will knew that Sylvie was behind him.

He turned. She leaned against the doorjamb, clinging to it, more like. Will had meant to be there before she put any pressure on that ankle.

He rushed to her side. "I didn't mean for you to have to walk on your ankle. I should have waited by the door."

She shrugged away from him. "You don't need to take care of me. I'm perfectly capable of taking care of myself. My ankle will be fine."

Will sensed she needed to convince herself more than him.

"Sure it will." He backed off. "But I still insist on doctoring your back. Why don't you sit down at the table." Will assisted her there, ignoring her attempt to limp on her own.

"Thanks." She turned her back to him and adjusted her shirt over her shoulder to expose the gash that ran from her shoulder to mid-back.

He winced. This was going to hurt.

Add to that, she was shaking all over. She'd had time to warm up, so it couldn't be from the cold. It must be a symptom of decompression sickness. She needed that hyperbaric chamber. And he was about to inflict more pain on her when he doctored this gash. He sent up a prayer, feeling helpless in all this.

Lord, when we are weak, You are strong. I need You to be strong for the both of us.

His prayer gave him a measure of peace. Sylvie could use some comfort and reassurance about now, too. But how did he give it?

Will grabbed the first-aid kit. He didn't like the look of the cut. It needed stitches. But he would do what he could and keep her talking so she wouldn't focus on the pain.

"I'm sorry for snapping at you," she said. "You don't deserve that. I'm just tired."

And injured. "No need to apologize. This has been a hard day for you."

"For you, too. You helped me, someone you didn't even know. Not too many would have done the same. Snake included."

Ah, so she'd been listening in longer than he thought. He was glad Snake had ventured outside for the moment.

"I'm nothing special so don't make me out to be."

"I can't say that I agree. Nor can I thank you enough for what you did today. What you're still doing."

"You're welcome."

"I heard you talking to Snake. He sounded upset with you for bringing me here. And what was he saying about five miles?"

She'd definitely heard more than he thought. No matter. He hadn't said anything he was ashamed of saying. "Don't worry about that for now." Will was glad he'd finished with her wound. "There, that should do it."

He made to stand, hoping to escape from her rush of questions. He didn't blame her, but he wasn't prepared to answer them fully until he figured things out. He needed to talk Snake out of the five-mile hike. And he needed to use the radio.

Will scooted the bowl of stew toward her. Sylvie grabbed him before he could get away. Heat danced up his arm from where she touched him. "I don't know how I'll ever repay you, but I'll find a way."

He already knew her well enough to expect that from her. She couldn't receive a kindness without needing to repay it. She thought she owed him. He eased his arm from her grip. "Don't worry about that. It's more important that you focus on staying alive."

More important that they find out who wanted to kill her. The same person who had already killed their mothers?

SIX

With warm stew in her stomach and a mesmerizing fire, Sylvie had never been more exhausted. The sofa was comfortable and broken in, and cocooned her, inviting her to sleep. She didn't want to close her eyes. After all, she was in an out-of-the-way cabin with two strangers. Two men she'd only known a few hours, never mind they had both been an intricate part of her survival so far.

When they figured out she was too exhausted to offer coherent conversation, they left her alone to rest—though she could still hear their hushed tones from the far side of the cabin where they practiced knife-throwing against a chunk of wood. Besides the shelf of old books against the wall, that could be Snake's only entertainment out here, and a necessary skill. Will's apparent expertise surprised her. She wouldn't want to face off with him. She remembered she'd lost his knife when she'd had to cut him out of the harness and swim him to shore.

Her gaze drifted to the diving equipment sitting out. It must belong to Snake. *Her* equipment was still in Will's plane. Had the doomed craft already sunk, never to be seen again—a reminder of the plane she'd come to find? At what point could they come back to retrieve her diving equipment? What did it matter? She couldn't get it in time to do her any good and might use Snake's gear to recompress herself. That was a seriously risky scenario that could kill her. She was counting on getting out of here at first light. Better to wait for the hyperbaric chamber in Juneau.

Will called her name out, jarring Sylvie awake. Somewhere behind his words, she heard a vibrating noise over the crackle of the fire in the otherwise quiet morning. That noise penetrated her catatonic state— and she forced herself to sit up, listen. Will stood at the open door, looking out, the gray of morning illuminating that portion of the cabin.

Whomp-whomp-whomp.

Realization dawned. A helicopter. Someone to rescue them.

Newfound energy surged through Sylvie. She eased from the sofa and limped over to where Will stood, hanging through the opening and letting the warm air out while the cold Alaska morning whipped inside and swirled around her feet.

Intent on listening, he didn't acknowledge her. She lifted her hand to touch his arm then dropped it when he tensed, as if he'd expected the touch. As if he hadn't wanted it.

"Why aren't you running out there to signal them?" Panic engulfed her. Sylvie pushed by, prepared to limp outside to wave at the helicopter. Will and Snake couldn't keep her here. "If you won't, then I will!"

"Sylvie, no." Will snatched her back.

Pain shot through her ankle. She screamed, hoping someone would hear her.

Will gripped her shoulders, his brown eyes imploring her to listen. "Last night I radioed Chief Winters with the Mountain Cove Police. He's someone I know and trust. Chief Winters is sending a SAR team to meet us at ten. That's not for another three hours. I figured it would take us that long to hike the terrain to the meet-up point, especially with your injured ankle. That helicopter isn't our help."

"How can you know that?"

"This isn't where I told them we'd be. And it doesn't sound like the type of chopper medevac uses. This is a single-engine. Small, maybe a two-seater."

She froze. "What are you saying?"

"I'm saying that I don't know who is flying the helicopter. Chief Winters didn't send this one."

"It could be someone who could help us. Someone willing to fly us to Juneau."

He pursed his lips. "Or it could be the men after you."

Sylvie backed away from him. "No, that can't be. How could they find us?"

"They could have spotted the plane sitting halfway out of the water if it hasn't already sunk. Then on foot they could have tracked us. Or the helicopter might be simply looking for smoke from the nearest cabin, knowing that would be our only shelter for miles."

"But how could they have found your plane? Covered that much ground without knowing where you were going?"

Will's eyes penetrated, stabbing at her core. "Easy enough. They could guess we were headed to Juneau and follow our general flight path. And if it's the men after you, you have to consider they're tracking you somehow. Maybe they put a tracker on your boat, or they're tracking your phone."

"I'm no longer on my boat and don't have my phone with me."

"Your diving gear, then. They found you in the channel and then could have followed you here. Your diving gear is on my plane. Maybe they figured I had landed, even if they didn't realize I crashed. But they've had enough time to get a helicopter and track you. So I don't want to risk it if it's them. Not when I know help that I trust is coming."

A tracking device on her diving gear? That was a frightening thought. And worse, it would mean that it was her fault if their attackers tracked her here, since she was the one who'd insisted on going back for her diving gear and loading it onto Will's plane. She didn't have time to think through the implications, not with Will's suspicious gaze on her. She'd told him she didn't know who was after her or why. And she didn't. Not really. But if they were together much longer, she'd need to share everything with him—what had driven her to search for the plane to begin with.

Will waited and listened, staring out the door, the porch both covering and hiding him from the searchers.

"Where's Snake?"

"He went out."

"You need to warn him."

"Don't worry. He won't be waving at the helicopter. If anything, he's angry that someone is looking for us and will inadvertently discover him."

A spray of bullets ricocheted through the woods. Will slammed the door and pressed his back against it. Determination carved his features. "We have to get out of here."

Scrambling around the cabin, he grabbed coats and packs that must have been prepared while Sylvie had slept. He tossed Sylvie a pair of Snake's boots. "Try those. They might be too big, but you need something to protect your feet besides the diving boots."

Sylvie understood the urgency and worked to put the boots on. There wasn't time to look for socks. It didn't matter if the boots didn't fit. But how could she run with her injured ankle?

The sound of the rotor blades drifted away.

"Do you think they'll come back?"

"They're not really gone. They're just looking for a place to land. They're onto us, Sylvie. They know we've taken refuge in this cabin."

"I'm surprised they didn't use a more stealth approach. They would have caught us off guard."

"It also would have taken longer, and they wouldn't want to give us a chance to get away." He pulled on his coat. "They're determined to find you. What haven't you told me, Sylvie?"

In the distance more automatic gunfire resounded outside, saving her from a reply. A big chunk of fear lodged in Sylvie's stomach. When would this end? She couldn't imagine it would end well.

Will went to the door and opened it.

"Wait! What are you doing? You can't go out there. You're going to get yourself killed."

"I have to find Snake. Make sure he's okay." Will grabbed a weapon off the table and chambered a round. He handed it to Sylvie. "You know how to use this?"

"Well enough." She didn't want it, but these were dire circumstances.

Once it was in her grip, she stared at it, a vise of fear squeezing her chest. Finally, she looked up at Will. All this she'd brought on him. On Snake. "Be careful."

Understanding passed between them. They were in this together. "Stay here and be ready to run when I get back."

Sylvie set the weapon on the table and sat in a chair to slip on Snake's boots. They rose above her midcalf and, if she tightened them enough, they just might be adequate support for her ankle so she could run.

She heard him outside on the porch. He hadn't left yet. Good. The too-big boots secured as much as possible. Sylvie shoved from the chair, pulled on the coat and opened the door to say words she'd never thought she'd say to anyone.

"Don't leave me!"

But Will had already disappeared through the woods to find Snake. She feared he would come face-to-face with the gunmen.

There was nothing he hated more than leaving Sylvie, but it couldn't be helped. He'd keep one eye on the cabin as he searched the nearby woods for Snake, who'd gone to one of the outbuildings. He should have returned by now.

When Will had first heard the helicopter, he'd tucked his borrowed weapon in his shoulder holster and prepared for what the next few moments would hold. And now he was in the thick of this fight for survival.

Hiding behind trees as he searched, he moved with

stealth through the woods, watching the cabin as he went. "Snake," he whispered loudly. "Where are you?"

The man could have taken off and left Will and Sylvie there to fend for themselves for all Will knew. But Will didn't want to believe it. The helicopter still hovered in the distance, confirming Will's belief the pilot was searching for a place to land or release someone who would soon come for them on foot. He couldn't be sure that someone wasn't already on the ground.

A glance back at the cabin told him no one had approached, but that could change at any moment. He had to get Sylvie out of there. Using the trees for cover, he searched for the missing man.

"Snake."

An ominous dark color surrounded a mound by the woodpile. Will's gut tightened. After another glance at the cabin and through the woods, he ran forward, dropped to his knees and searched for a pulse. But the wound in Snake's head and the blood-stained ground told him enough.

"No…" Will cried. Acid burned his throat. "No, God, why?"

Snake's death was his fault. He shouldn't have brought Sylvie here, but he hadn't known it would end like this.

He said a quick prayer over Snake then, "I'm sorry, Snake. Real sorry."

Will pushed to his feet and scraped the raw emotion from his face, letting anger and determination push up and drive him forward. He hefted Snake in a fireman's carry and trudged to the cabin. He'd have to get to Juneau before he could organize a funeral for the man, but until then, he wouldn't leave his body to the wolves.

Wolves came in many different forms.

When he made it to the cabin, the door opened and Sylvie stood there wide-eyed and waiting.

"What happened?"

"They got Snake. We have to leave now. I heard them landing."

"I'm so sorry." Sylvie looked as if she would cry, but ran her hand across her eyes and swiped the emotions away.

"No time for regrets. If we want to live we have to go." Will looked her over. "Looks like you're ready. The temperature is dropping. We have at least three hours to hike and evade capture while we wait for a rescue. Grab the packs. I'm going to use the radio one last time." He went to the small room where Snake kept his Ham radio. Again, old school, but Chief Winters kept one, as well.

Will made the call and warned Chief Winters what had happened so he could bring backup and understand the urgency and danger they would face. Will wasn't sure how long he and Sylvie could last, but knowing that others were on their way to help bolstered his confidence. He had a smidgen of hope they would survive.

It didn't last long. Not when he heard what the chief had to say next.

He finished on the radio and hung his head.

"What's wrong?" Sylvie asked from behind.

"Their helicopter was diverted to another emergency and delayed. Chief Winters promises to find other resources for us and send them as soon as possible. For obvious reasons, I can't hang out at the radio and call someone else for help."

He left the room and grabbed one of the packs that Sylvie had set next to the sofa. Snake had prepared food and supplies for them. Will scrambled to put it on as Sylvie did hers. Wait. Will had to carry Sylvie instead of the pack. Snake was supposed to carry one of them and now he was gone.

Sylvie leaned against the sofa and watched him. "What are we going to do?"

"We're going to survive." He refused to let her see the fear that gripped him. Only his determination to stay alive.

"You ready?"

She nodded.

"Let's go."

He tried to assist her, let her lean against him to walk across the cabin, but she shrugged out of his reach. "I can do this."

He'd let her think that until they had to run. For now it was awfully quiet out there. Will peeked through the door, weapon at the ready. They would be most vulnerable leaving the cabin, but he'd stay close to the trees. Snake had done well in using the canopy to hide this place, though the smoke from the chimney had most decidedly given them away to anyone bent on finding them. But all they had to do was stay alive just long enough to make their rendezvous—and hope that help would actually arrive, as planned.

Before he opened the door wide, he looked at Sylvie. "We're going to make a run for it. And you might not like this."

Her eyes grew wary. "What?"

"I'm going to carry you piggyback style. It's the best way for me to run and make good time and get us out of danger."

Sylvie opened her mouth to argue then shut it. She blew out a breath. "Okay."

"All we have to do is stay alive long enough. Help is on the way. They're coming for us." Just not as fast as Will had hoped.

He'd never had to run for his life. Never had to protect someone or help them this way. He never wanted anyone to depend on him like Sylvie depended on him, though she'd never admit to that. But he could see the uncertainty and apprehension in her eyes—beautiful hazel eyes that he wanted to look at again under much different circumstances.

Knock it off.

Will opened the door and positioned her on his back. "Are you okay? Am I hurting you?"

"No. I'm fine."

But he heard the discomfort in her voice. She wouldn't tell him she was in pain.

A bullet slammed into the log next to his head.

They were out of time.

SEVEN

Sylvie fought the scream that exploded in her throat.

Will slammed the door shut. Ignoring her ankle, Sylvie slipped down to let him catch his breath. He pressed his back against the door.

"God, we could use some help here," he said between gasps. "They're a good distance away so we have this one chance to escape the cabin."

After gesturing her out of the way, he motioned for her to duck down. "Be ready to run."

Then he opened the door again to deliver a round of bullets. He slammed the door and picked her up and ran to the back of the cabin. He set her gently against the wall as if she were porcelain.

"We have seconds before they make the cabin."

She gulped a breath. "How many... How many are there?"

"I don't know." Will struggled with the window. "Two maybe."

She hoped he didn't make too much noise so they'd focus on the front door. "Before, there were only two men. Diverman and Rifleman." That she knew about. Had there been someone equally murderous driving the boat? And obviously, someone had stolen *her* boat, moving it out of her reach. Destroying the evidence she'd even been there.

Will finally got the window open then quietly slipped through, watching the woods as he assisted her out. The trees made good cover here, if nothing else. But then there was an open patch they had to cross. Sylvie followed him through the window, ignoring her pain, bruises and scratches from yesterday. What did any of her injuries matter if someone shot her in the head like Snake?

Once she climbed through the window, Will let her scramble onto his back again and then he sprinted as though she weighed nothing, which she knew wasn't true. She might be small, but her solid frame made her weigh more than other women her size.

By the time he made it across the small clearing between the cabin and outbuildings and into the thick cover of woods, Will was breathing hard. He stopped behind a big tree for cover and panted. Sylvie wanted her freedom from the position on his back but knew to keep quiet. They weren't out of trouble yet and she wasn't sure they would ever be until help came.

He crept forward between the trees, putting distance between them and Snake's cabin. She'd brought danger to Snake that had killed him—a man who'd chosen to live away from civilization. Her stomach soured. It never should have happened.

She couldn't let it happen to Will. She tried to watch the woods to help him, but twisting her neck around while she jostled on his back made her dizzy. Neither did she want a bullet in the back. Maybe the pack she wore would provide protection enough. Will stepped into a brook and waded upstream, getting his boots wet. She wasn't sure how far they'd gone when he stepped out of the brook and paused in the crack of a bluff between large boulders. When he set her down, she collapsed onto soft, mossy ground and shrugged out of the backpack.

He plopped down next to her, his face drawn tight. "Are you okay?" he whispered.

She nodded.

To her surprise, he ran a finger down her cheek, picking something off. A leaf, dirt, she wasn't sure, but something in his gesture made it feel as though he cherished Sylvie. That couldn't be true. Nor did she want that from him or anyone. Unfortunately, her heart jumped at his touch no matter her personal resolve.

"What are we going to do?" she asked.

"We can hike to town if we have to."

Right. She blew out a breath. Like she would believe that. Time to face the truth. "Even if that were true, it won't take them long to track us. We're too slow and we can't outrun them. We can't make it to town before they find us."

"Then we'll just stay alive until help arrives." Will leaned in closer until his face was inches from hers. So he could lower his voice? "Do you trust me?"

His brown eyes seemed to caress her. His masculine scent—a woodsy mixture of loam and pure, wild adrenaline—grew heady and wrapped around her until she couldn't breathe. She struggled to speak. "I don't know."

She couldn't rely on anyone but herself. Still, she wanted to trust Will. Just how far, she wasn't sure.

His brows knit together.

"I trust you to do your best, but don't lie to me about our chances. I'm grateful for all you've done, but I don't see how we're going to make it."

Hurt spilled from his gaze. He eased back, pulled his weapon out. "Have a little faith, will you?"

"I've never had anyone shoot at me before, have you?"

"No." He angled his head to listen. Through the opening between the boulders he watched the woods.

She didn't like this position. They were trapped. Someone could ambush them. What was he thinking by stopping here?

When he turned back, the warmth had returned to his eyes, but under it was a cold resolve that hadn't been there before. It scared her. This wasn't the Will she'd come to know in a few short hours. Was this experience changing him, like it changed her? And yet, how could it not?

"What are you thinking?" she asked, not at all sure she wanted to hear his answer.

Drawing a breath, he worked his jaw. She was close enough she could feel the muscles in his shoulders tense. "I've never had anyone shoot at me. Nor have I ever shot at someone until today. And I've never—" he exhaled long and hard "—killed another human being."

He hung his head, and once again Sylvie held her breath even with her heart pounding wildly. "Will." Her whisper was a mere croak.

He lifted his eyes to hers. The way he held her gaze, searched for something inside her, Sylvie almost thought he was trying to decide if she was worth the cost, but then she knew he'd already found that answer. He'd claimed that he was just doing what anyone else would have by rescuing her yesterday, but he was going far beyond what she ever could have expected from a stranger. And Sylvie had the strangest sensation that this moment in time bonded them together forever. Gave them a connection like no other. She didn't want to be that close to anyone or dependent on them. She saw where that had gotten her mother. But at that moment her connection to Will was her lifeline, and it went far deeper than she cared to admit.

Whatever the bond, he broke it with his next words. "My father taught me everything I know about weapons. Told me if you're going to learn how to shoot a gun, you'd better be prepared to use it."

Sylvie wasn't sure she liked where this conversation was going. Her insides quaked, but at the same time she resigned herself to the fact that they might have to kill to survive. "Meaning?"

"I will protect you, Sylvie. Whatever it takes. Whatever that means. If it comes to that, I'll kill for you."

His words elicited dread in her eyes. He wanted her to believe in him, believe they could survive this. The words were meant for him as much as for her. He had to speak out his resolve, let it sink in. When he'd fired his weapon from the cabin, he hadn't been aiming at anything or anyone in particular. The shots had been meant to deter their pursuers. He wasn't in a position to make a kill shot then anyway.

But if they were on their own, if help wouldn't come soon enough, Will would cover ground, as much as possible. Then he'd lie in wait and make the kill if it came to that.

"We need to keep moving." He hoped they hadn't rested too long. "You ready?"

"No, I'm not. How long do we keep running?"

"Until it's over." His tone had turned brusque. He didn't recognize himself at the moment. But he didn't like the feeling that death was swooping down on them like a raptor just waiting for the right moment to stick its claws in.

He peered from behind the boulder. Watched and listened. Patches of light dappled the woods. At least it wasn't raining at the moment. The thick greenery was tranquil except for birdsong and skittering small animals through brush. A red squirrel darted into Will and Sylvie's hiding place between the boulders then back out. They probably stood too near where the creature had stashed acorns. They'd leave soon enough and the squirrel could get to his stash.

If the woods could be trusted, there didn't seem to be any sign of their assailants.

In the distance a twig snapped, and a hush fell over the forest. Even the breeze dropped. Another snap and it almost sounded as if the man had taken a wrong turn. Was going in the wrong direction. That would give Will and Sylvie a chance.

After he positioned Sylvie so they could make good time, he crept quietly, slowly, from behind the boulder. Relief washed through him. No answering gunfire was there to meet them. And yet he couldn't afford to let down his guard for even a second.

They were still a few minutes away from making their original meeting place. He could have asked help to come to the cabin, but he and Sylvie couldn't outlast a gun battle there and would be long dead by the time help arrived. So he'd kept to his original plan, hoping he could evade their pursuers and arrive around the same time as their rescuers.

He'd asked that they come as soon as possible.

Now he wished he would have begged.

Come on, Chief Winters, where's the helicopter? Where's our rescue? Didn't I make it clear we were on the run from killers?

Not clear enough, apparently. Will's back and legs ached, but he kept moving toward the rendezvous point and in the opposite direction of the men after Sylvie. At least he hoped.

Finally, Will was spent. The muscles in his arms had been cramping for an hour. Still, even carrying a woman on his back, over rough and difficult terrain, they had made good time.

He let Sylvie off his back and nestled her against the thick trunk of a Hemlock. Moss grew at its base along with the vast greenery found in the temperate rainforest. He wished for the bluff with the boulders. That had been good, quiet and safe cover. But they could hide here, too, melt into the forest and wait it out until their rescue helicopter came.

Will leaned against the tree and hung his head to catch his breath. Gather his composure before she looked too long and hard at his face and saw the truth. Sylvie reached up and squeezed his arm. Reassurance?

"Thank you," she whispered.

He peered at her. Those hazel eyes would get to him every time. "Don't thank me yet."

"Are we going to keep moving? What's the plan?"

"No. We stay here. This is our rendezvous point—or near enough. But we need good cover until help comes.

When we hear *our* helicopter, we'll make a run for the meadow up a ways where it can land. From here, though, if we must, we hold our ground."

She held up Snake's weapon, a grin contrasting the somber expression in her eyes. "Like in an old shoot-'em-up movie."

"Something like that, but let's hope we don't have to get into a shoot-out." He hoped all that was left to do was wait and watch. Wait for the rescue helicopter. Watch for their assailants. He perused the woods. Heard nothing. Saw nothing.

"Right, because I'm no marksman."

"I don't know how many there are but I suspect two. Three at the most, but I'm hoping for one. I should be able to pick them off if I see them in time."

Admiration filled her eyes, surprising him. Something warm tugged at him, fighting to get inside, but Will wouldn't let it. He didn't like that he cared what she thought about him. Until that moment, he hadn't realized her opinion of him mattered. He wouldn't let himself give in to the draw of her beauty, both inside and out. No, Sylvie wasn't a manipulator like Michelle had been. Far from it. But that didn't mean Will would allow himself to be vulnerable again.

"You're full of surprises, Will Pierson."

"There's more where that came from." He didn't just say that.

"What do you mean?" She angled her head.

He paused before he answered, listening to their surroundings and watching the forest for signs of the men after them. Prickles crawled over him.

A bullet pinged against the tree above Will's head. "Get down!"

Then another cracked the bark.

Will peered around the tree.

Aimed.

Fired twice.

The man ducked out of sight.

Again, Will watched and waited. He prayed they could get out of here without facing off with the men, but that was not to be. How many men were out there? Just the one he'd spotted, or were there more? He couldn't be sure. After too much time had gone by without any more sound or movement, he thought he should check and see if he'd injured the man. He hadn't shot to kill, would only take that step if there was no other choice. Instead, he was holding on to that one last hope their help would arrive and capture the men. He and Sylvie could get their answers that way.

But he'd protect her at all costs.

"Sylvie," he whispered.

She didn't answer.

"Sylvie?"

Will held his weapon steady but glanced behind him. She was slumped over. Will dropped his weapon and grabbed her, spotting a hole in her coat. He tugged it off her shoulder and down her arm.

There, red spread across her shirt. A lightning bolt of pain struck Will's heart.

"Oh, no, please, no…"

He tugged the shirt open and found the gunshot wound through her shoulder, blood gushing out. His whole body shook at the sight. Ignoring the cold, he tugged off his coat and then shirt, pressing it against Sylvie's wound. He prayed the bullet hadn't nicked an artery, but this heavy bleeding told him otherwise.

I have to stop the bleeding.

"Sylvie, please don't die on me, please don't die."
Bile erupted in Will's throat.

*God, where is the rescue helicopter? Please, don't
let me down.*

But *Will* had let *Sylvie* down. He told her that he'd
protect her and keep her safe but his shots had been too
little and too late. Her life poured from her, the shirt
he'd used saturated with it. His hands were covered in
her blood. Emotion burning behind his eyes, his heart
tripped up, tumbled over.

She wasn't going to make it.

EIGHT

The world spun around him—the trees and sky swirled, the brook trickled too loudly from a distance—then time seemed to slow along with the whop of rotor blades from the helicopter hovering above him.

Panic crawled over Will.

Was it their help arriving at last? Or the enemy helicopter? Will grappled with the sound, trying to recognize the kind of bird, but his focus was shot. His hands slicked with Sylvie's blood, he grabbed his weapon, ready to protect her, defend her. But his head told his heart he was too late. He'd already failed.

Two men lowered from the helicopter. Faces he recognized. Cade Warren and a paramedic whose name failed him. He couldn't comprehend their words as they pushed him back and away from Sylvie.

"No, stay away from her!" He yanked Cade away. But what was he doing?

Cade gripped Will's shoulders, pinned him against the tree and removed the weapon from Will's grasp. "We're here to help. Get a grip, man. You're in shock."

Compassion eased into Cade's expression. "Are you good?"

Stunned at the words, the truth of them, Will squeezed his eyes. "Yeah, yeah. I'm good. Just save her. Save her…"

He prayed that the world would quit tilting on him. "God, save Sylvie."

I thought I could save her. That I could protect her. She was right next to me, behind me, practically. Behind the tree. And still, I let her get shot, and now she's fighting for her life. How…how did this happen?

The next thing Will knew, they hoisted a basket holding Sylvie to the helicopter. Cade remained behind. Another man—a police officer—stood nearby, his gun drawn. How or when had he gotten there?

"Is she going to make it?" Will hung his head, seeing the blood-stained moss at the tree's base. Would he ever forget that image? When Cade didn't answer, Will lifted his gaze.

His expression grim, Cade said, "I don't know."

"When gunfire erupted, I returned fire. I wasn't aiming to kill. Not yet. Just trying to hold out until you guys arrived. But the man never fired back. There was no movement. I need to know if I killed him. Or…if he's injured." Will should have thought of that and already informed Cade. He was failing miserably. "There was another helicopter that fired on us earlier—that killed John Snake, the man who gave us shelter last night. That's why I pulled my gun on you. There could be more men. I can't be sure."

"We don't have much time." Cade signaled the Mountain Cove officer. "Chief Winters sent one of his men in lieu of the troopers. He was afraid we wouldn't get here in time if we had to wait."

And they almost hadn't anyway. Will pushed away

from the tree and hurried to the place where the man had been shooting from, Cade and the officer on his heels. There was nothing, no one, next to the tree. Will hadn't seen anyone coming or going. What use was he in protecting Sylvie? None. He let his gaze roam the area. The rescue helicopter must have sent the man running.

"And Snake. His body is in the cabin. We need to get it."

Cade shook his head. "Don't worry, we'll come back for Snake. This woman's life is on the line. We need to go and now!"

Cade led the way back to where the helicopter still hovered, and the three of them were each lifted into the craft. As the helicopter flew over the forest, Will looked outside, searching the woods for their attackers. He looked anywhere but at Sylvie, where two medics worked on her. Isaiah Callahan, Cade's brother-in-law, flew the helicopter. Will almost wished he would have stayed to find who had done this. Or that the police officer would have stayed to search for evidence. They could have done Sylvie more good on the ground.

But it was too late now. There was nothing left to do except pray. Will squeezed his eyes and hung his head, trying to shove aside his own guilt in what happened, and his concern and worry over Sylvie.

Just have a little faith.

Hadn't he told her the same?

Cade nudged him. "Sorry it took us so long, man."

Will didn't want to hear excuses. Angry with them, angry with himself, he couldn't respond. Time stretched on and took far too long to get to the nearest hospital where Sylvie could get the blood she needed to survive and a hyperbaric chamber to resolve the decompression sickness.

"Who is she?" Cade asked.

"Sylvie Masters." It hit him then. He sucked in a breath, pulled his gaze from the terrain below and stared at Cade.

He doesn't know that she's his half sister.

Cade didn't realize. *Oh, Lord, help me...* Will didn't want to betray her trust—the promise she'd extracted from him—but Cade needed to know.

"What is it?"

God, what do I do? Do I tell him? Will Sylvie speak to me again?

Will pressed the heels of his palms in his eyes. "Okay, this isn't for me to share, but maybe she'll understand."

"Tell me."

"You have to keep this to yourself. Can you do that?"

"Depends, Will, you know that."

"Yeah, well, try to keep this under wraps for her sake. Sylvie Masters is Regina Hemphill's daughter. The child she conceived with your father before she left Mountain Cove."

Will stared at Cade, watching as his pupils dilated, as realization knocked him back into his seat, pinned him against it. The man's expression morphed, pain etching his features when he glanced over at the woman fighting for her life.

Finally, an exhale burst from his lips along with, "She's my half sister."

Light filtered into her dreams, stirring her awake. Sylvie wanted to open her eyes but her lids were heavy.

Nor could she move or lift her arms. Was something pressed on top of her, holding her down? No, it was more that she had no strength. She wondered how she could have survived the freight train that had obviously barreled over her.

"Sylvie." A familiar male voice wrapped around her. "You're going to be okay. You're going to wake up soon and everything is going to be fine."

Where was she? Sylvie frowned. At least she could do that much.

"Sylvie, please, wake up."

An image came into her mind. The face that belonged to the voice. Who was he?

"Will?" her voice croaked out, sounding as if it had come from down a long, dark tunnel. As if it had come from someone else.

A large hand with a strong grip squeezed hers. She squeezed back.

"Can you hear me?" he asked.

Sylvie's eyelids fluttered and she found the strength to open them—though she could already tell that keeping them open would be a problem. She looked at Will now, the details of his handsome face coming into sharp focus. Only he looked beaten up, haggard in a way she hadn't remembered. What had happened to him?

"You're awake." His grin thrilled her, but concern, as well as delight, poured from his gaze.

Now she started to remember. His brown eyes taking her in when she climbed into his plane. The wariness in them the first time she'd seen him. There was a tug at her heart that he was there with her now. She was glad to see him, but wasn't sure why. Who was he to her? What was wrong with her that she couldn't remember?

She drew in a ragged breath, unsure how much energy she had left to keep her eyes open much less speak. "Where am I?"

His grin quickly faded, but he squeezed her hand again. "You're in the hospital. They're taking good care of you."

"What happened?" She had to know. Had to remember before she lost her strength.

"You lost a lot of blood." He inched closer. "Sylvie, I'm so sorry."

"How long… How long have I been here?"

"Two days. You're going to be fine. They say it will take you some time to regain your strength. You had a mild case of DCS, and with the gunshot wound it was complicated."

"Oh, right." She'd needed the hyperbaric chamber, but…gunshot wound?

And why was Will here instead of her stepfather? Sylvie tensed, hoping they hadn't known to contact him, or hadn't been able to reach him since he was out of the country.

Sylvie felt herself drifting in and out, and Will's voice, his face, did the same.

"You should rest."

Will said nothing more, and Sylvie's sluggish mind took time to process the words. Soak up his presence. Something about him sitting next to her gave her a sense of security, though she struggled to understand why she needed it. Then the horror came rushing back and she wished it hadn't. Wished she could feel safe with Will without the harsh memories of the attacks against her.

A nurse entered the room and insisted Sylvie needed to rest, confirming Will's suggestion. She didn't want to release Will's hand, let go of the strength there, but he pulled away from her. Sylvie wanted to look in his eyes, let the warmth there wash away the disquiet in her heart, but her lids betrayed her. Then darkness replaced light.

When Sylvie awoke again, she found two men in her room. Fear jumped down her throat, then Will stepped forward. She hoped he would reach for her hand again, but he didn't.

His grin, revealing a couple of dimples, could make her feel better, but his eyes weren't convincing.

What was wrong?

"How are you feeling?" he asked.

I'd be better if you'd sit close to me and hold my hand. But she couldn't say that. She hated how vulnerable and needy she'd become.

A nurse came in and repositioned her pillow and bed so she could sit up. She brought her a tray of hospital food. Sylvie had no appetite. She felt uncomfortable with the stranger and waited for Will's explanation. When the nurse left them alone, he stepped closer. He looked as though he hadn't slept in days. How long had she been here? She got the sense that he hadn't left her side, but she was certain she was just fooling herself. She couldn't be that important to him.

"The police are going to question you soon," he said.

She turned her hand over, hoping he'd take it. It hadn't required a conscious thought, simply reflexive need. And Will, apparently attuned to her subtle needs, took her hand. She wasn't sure what she felt about her desires or his response to them.

"I don't think I'm coherent enough to answer questions."

"Do you remember that you were shot?"

She shook her head. "I'm not sure. I remember cling-ing to the tree as gunfire erupted. Everything is blurry after that."

"I tried to protect you but he shot you."

"Who, Will? Who shot me?"

"I don't know. I fired back, but he got away. We think the rescue helicopter sent him running."

"The police are hoping you can give some answers about who might be trying to kill you." The man stand-ing in the shadowed corner of the room finally spoke.

Was he with the police? Sylvie let her gaze travel to him.

Will chose that moment to sit on the edge of the bed. It seemed like such an intimate gesture for a man she hardly knew, but they'd been through something to-gether. She had a bond with him and struggled to re-member what it was. He'd stayed with her through this; she believed that. Why couldn't she remember more?

"I'm sorry, but I couldn't keep it from him."

"What are you talking about?"

"When our helicopter came and the rescuers hoisted us up, I had to share your secret with him because… well, I thought you were…" Will hung his head. "I thought you were dying."

Dying…

She had almost died?

"What secret, Will? You're scaring me."

"Please forgive me for telling him, but I believed the circumstances warranted full disclosure."

The man stepped closer. With the deep set of his woodsy-green eyes, thick head of dark-roasted-coffee hair and his good, strong features, the face was somehow familiar, and yet she was sure she had never met this man.

"Sylvie." His grin was big and welcoming to an extent that seemed inappropriate coming from a stranger. "I'm glad to finally meet you. My name is Cade Warren."

Ah, now she understood the grin. And the sense of familiarity. Her heart beat wildly. She wasn't ready for this. What did she say to him? This wasn't how she'd wanted to meet him, if she'd ever been ready to make that leap. And Will, it seemed, couldn't be trusted with secrets. She thought to glare at him, but she couldn't take her eyes from her half sibling in the flesh. A weight pressed against her chest. She was bungling this first meeting, and badly, with her reaction. Or rather, trying to hide her reaction to him.

Pain flickered in his eyes but compassion quickly took its place. "I'm your half brother."

"I know who you are." She hesitated. "I just don't know what to say. How to feel."

Despite her clumsy words, he tossed her another easy smile and she finally relaxed.

"I know this is a shock for you. It's a lot to happen at once." He grabbed Will's shoulder and squeezed. "And please don't blame Will, but I was there on the scene to get you guys, and well…we weren't sure if you would make it. Will didn't think it was right for him to keep your identity from me."

"I understand. I…I just wasn't ready for this. For any of it." For someone trying to kill her. For meeting Cade Warren. "I had dreamed of meeting you under different circumstances."

Now Sylvie could finally offer her own smile, begging for some grace. By his demeanor and the look in his gaze, she believed he gave her the understanding she needed and much more.

"I can't keep this to myself, you understand. I need to share the news with the rest of the family."

"Are you sure you don't resent me? That *they* won't resent me? After all, learning about my existence couldn't have been pleasant. The circumstances under which I was born…" Sylvie regretted her words. They must open the wound even deeper.

Cade held up a hand to keep her from saying more. "None of that is your fault. I don't blame you. None of us do. We can't change the past, so we'll all go forward and celebrate that we can finally meet and, hopefully, get to know you. I know the family will want to meet you as soon as I tell them."

She blew out a breath, rested her head against the pillow. "Not yet, please. Give me some time. When I came to southeast Alaska, I was looking for my mother. Other than my stepfather, she was my only family, and now she's gone. It's a bit overwhelming to suddenly have brothers and sisters." Though she'd known for years she had them, and now she wondered why it had taken so long for her to find the courage to connect. She hadn't initiated the meeting today, and she wasn't sure she ever would have.

"And a grandmother, and brother- and sisters-in-law, nephews and a niece on the way," Cade added with a smile. "I'll give you some time, let's say a day tops. But they'll kill me if I keep this news from them for very long."

"I understand." He owed more to his family, the brothers and sister he'd grown up with, than he did to her. "But when you do tell them, no one else can know. No one besides family. Agreed?"

"Agreed. You take care of yourself." Cade glanced from her to Will, his smile still in place. "I'll leave you two alone now."

As he left, she almost missed his subtle wink at Will, as if he thought there was something going on between them.

Sylvie rubbed her arms, careful of the IV. How could Cade truly be so gracious? After all, she was the daughter of his father's mistress. And was his acceptance of her real? Meeting the guy in person, she had a hard time believing he was anything but completely up front. Otherwise, why even come here and introduce himself? But what about the others? Would they be so anxious to meet her? So willing to receive her?

"I've already talked to the police." Will's soft words broke through her chaotic thoughts. "Given them my statement. They're going to ask you a lot more questions." Will's expression grew somber. "Before things get crazy around here, I want you to know that I'm in this with you for the long haul. I can't help but think the men after you wanted to stop you from finding the plane. Finding your mother. And my mother. And if that's the case then the plane crash wasn't an accident. Is that what you believe?"

"Yes." Sylvie had suspected all along that it wasn't an accident because of the words her mother had said to her before she left. But she needed to find the plane.

"We're in this together. I want to help you find out who tried to kill you. And what happened to that plane carrying precious cargo."

Precious cargo. Her and Will's mothers.

"Tried to kill *us*, Will. Not just me. Now that you're part of this, your life is in danger, too. I'm sorry this happened to you. That I involved you." Since he was involved, she needed to tell him everything. But how? She wasn't sure she could trust him with everything. "Thanks again for coming back for me on the island."

"I'm not sorry I'm involved," he said. "I'm just glad I was there when you needed someone. Even knowing the danger, I would do it over again, Sylvie."

Sylvie didn't have time to ponder his meaning. Two Alaska State Troopers stepped into her room and sent Will on his way.

NINE

While in Snake's cabin, Will had contacted those he trusted, and the North Face Search and Rescue team—including Cade Warren—had responded along with someone from the Mountain Cove PD. But they weren't the ones investigating the crimes now. The Alaska State Troopers were the law-enforcement entity to ask the questions. The crimes had happened outside Mountain Cove and even the large area encompassing Juneau's jurisdiction, but there were no county sheriffs in Alaska.

Even though the Alaska State Troopers were officially in charge, Will would also share everything that had happened with Mountain Cove Police Chief Winters. What happened to Sylvie and Will, this investigation, somehow involved Will's mother. If he followed through with this line of thinking, she had been murdered right alongside Sylvie's mother. But what Will couldn't be sure about was which one of the mothers was the target and which one was the accidental victim. Or had they both been caught up in something together that had gotten them killed? His mother, Margaret Pierson, had been a citizen of Mountain Cove since she and his father had moved there from Montana three decades ago. Chief Winters should be kept informed on everything about her murder so he could do his own investigation if warranted.

After Will sipped the last of the vending-machine coffee, he crushed the paper cup and tossed it, growing impatient with the troopers to finish taking down Sylvie's statement. He had a burning question of his own. Would Sylvie share anything more with the police than she'd shared with Will?

If Will went with his gut on this, then he thought Sylvie had suspected her mother had been murdered long before men had come onto the scene and tried to kill her. The attack just confirmed her suspicions. It was those initial suspicions that had sent her looking for the plane.

What did she know? What or whom did she suspect was responsible?

Or maybe Will was wrong and Sylvie knew more but didn't realize it. But that didn't seem likely, either. Sylvie was smart. No. She knew something about that plane and was holding it close. Was she protecting someone?

He didn't like being played or manipulated, but to be fair, Sylvie hardly knew him. Why should she trust him? Except they had this one strange connection, this one thing in common.

Their mothers had both died together in that crash.

That gave Will a reason to see her again. He'd already told her that he'd help her find out what had happened to their mothers. Still, his reasons for wanting to see her again went beyond the precarious situation they found themselves in together. The thought took him by surprise.

But Will couldn't follow through. He'd already suffered with the deep pain that came from experiencing a shattered heart. If remembering the pain from his past wasn't enough to keep his heart safe, he'd simply remind himself that Sylvie hated to fly. He got up every morning eager to meet the sky. Nothing inspired him more than drifting or soaring in the air through wide-open spaces, over the lofty snow-covered peaks of Alaska, or dipping deep into the valleys and seeing the fjords and waterfalls.

Nothing better than soaring with the eagles where the sky had no limits.

Nothing inspired him more. He would never give that up. No sense in falling for another woman who disdained his greatest joy. Will didn't have time to ponder more when the two Alaska State Troopers exited Sylvie's room.

Will kept his distance. He didn't want to be dragged into more questions for which he had no answers. Plus, he figured she would need a few minutes to compose herself. He had needed that himself. They had to have drained her with their interrogation, as they had him, and he hadn't been recovering from a gunshot wound or decompression sickness. He hadn't lost so much blood that he'd almost died.

The thought sent his mind back to their narrow escape through the woods behind Snake's cabin, and then to the tree behind which they'd taken cover. To the gunshots fired and to Sylvie nearly bleeding to death. Shaking the morbid thoughts away, Will thanked the Lord for Sylvie's life. In the waiting area, he stayed in the shadowed corner a little longer and sent up another prayer for the Lord's protection. They were going to need it. Until these men were caught, they were both in danger.

Will opened his eyes in time to see a male nurse enter her room. The man's scrubs pulled tight across his chest and over large biceps as he glanced both ways down the hall before he closed the door. Will frowned. Something didn't feel right. He might be too paranoid after everything they'd been through, but he always listened to his instincts.

He shoved from the wall and headed to her room, wondering why the Alaska State Troopers hadn't thought to post an officer by her door. Asking them would be Will's next order of business after he checked on her. Will opened the door and stepped inside the room.

Sylvie slept, looking exhausted and fragile. The nurse prepared a syringe presumably to stick in Sylvie's IV, adding medication to the drip. His gaze flicked to Will—and something in the man's eyes sent warnings through Will's head. Yeah, it was always in the eyes.

Will edged close to the man, getting in his space, preparing for a negative reaction. "What's that you're giving her? She's already asleep."

The nurse threw a fist at Will but he ducked in time. Adrenaline surging, Will launched at the brawny man, pulling him away from Sylvie as he tried to insert the needle into Sylvie's arm instead of the drip. Will had him in a choke hold but still the syringe edged dangerously close to Sylvie's arm.

"Help!" Will yelled. "Sylvie, wake up."

She needed to help him fight for her life.

With every ounce of strength he could muster, Will pulled the man back away from the hospital bed, and he fell on top of Will, knocking the air from him. But at least the syringe slid across the floor and out of reach. Will would crush it. Destroy what had to be a deadly poison.

Except the man posing as a nurse climbed off Will and pulled out a gun.

He aimed at Sylvie. She was awake now, her eyes wide with terror as she screamed. Will scrambled to his feet and shoved the weapon's trajectory away from Sylvie, aware that if the gun went off, it could very well go through a wall and injure another patient or hospital staff. He didn't want that, but neither would he let this man kill Sylvie.

Will wrestled to gain control of the thick-necked bouncer man again, trying to force him to release the gun by twisting the man's arm back and over the corner of the nightstand. The weapon fired.

Once.

Twice.

Three times.

A cacophony of screams erupted, echoing through his ringing ears.

God, help me! Protect Sylvie. Protect us all.

Muscles straining, sweat beaded his forehead. But he wouldn't let the man shoot Sylvie. "Get out of here, Sylvie. If you can, get out."

She tried to move from the bed to escape, but in her weakened condition she collapsed to the floor. Releasing a grunt, Will shoved the man against the wall, slamming his arm and pinning him, crushing his wrist until the man cried out and the weapon fell. Strong though he was, the man wasn't as motivated to kill Sylvie as Will was to save her life.

Will kicked the weapon across the floor against the wall.

The man growled and twisted out of Will's grip then shoved Will out of the way before running out the door.

Breathing hard, Will glanced at Sylvie, who'd crawled to the corner of the room. "I'm all right," she said.

A nurse rushed in as Will exited. "Take care of her and call security, call the police if you haven't already."

"Will!" Sylvie called. "Don't go!"

Her words knifed through him. He didn't want to leave her, but neither could he let this man get away. Instead, he rushed into the hallway, quickly spotting the man who was shoving doctors, nurses and hospital staff along with their carts, out of his way, leaving screams and clattering trays in his wake. Security guards appeared at the opposite end of the hallway. Of course. They would never catch up. Will gave chase and followed him down the hall. He pushed through the doors into the stairwell a mere ten seconds behind the man.

Hastening footsteps echoed through the stairwell below. Will continued his pursuit, wishing he had a weapon, or that he had grabbed the man's gun even though he knew that same weapon could get Will killed when the security officers or police caught up. Still, why was he the one giving chase? Where were the police when you needed them? Frustration churned in his gut, propelling him forward.

He had to catch this guy. Couldn't let him get away, or he might try to hurt Sylvie again. Lungs burning, he flew down the steps, taking more at a time than was safe. Another door opened and slammed shut. Will peered over the banister and saw nothing. But there was only one exit. He reached the last floor and shoved through into another hallway where it was obvious the man had torn a reckless path through hospital staff and bewildered patients.

"Where did he go?"

Visitors and nursing staff stared at him, their eyes wide and mouths hanging open.

Will kept running, following the trail of destruction, and peered through every door that would open as he went. Nothing. "Please, somebody help me. Did you see which way he went? I need to catch him."

A brunette staffer pointed. "Out the door."

He nodded his thanks as he passed. *God, please don't let me lose him.*

When he ran out into an alley he found a garbage receptacle and a delivery truck. Will carefully searched as he ran down the alley and into a hospital driveway, the visitor parking lot across the road. Catching his breath, he turned, searching the area for the man running from him. Cars came and went along the street that encircled the hospital. Could the man be driving one of them, making his escape?

Will sagged in defeat. He'd been so close. *How could I have lost him?*

Someone shoved through the door behind Will. A security guard. He looked at Will ready to pounce.

Will had to deflect those thoughts immediately. "He got away," Will said. "Drove off. Disguised himself. Melted into the walls. I don't know."

He could still be in the hospital for all Will knew. Sylvie needed 24/7 protection. Someone was willing to go to great lengths to kill her, and there could be no doubt that they would be back.

They would keep trying until they succeeded.

Sylvie sat on the edge of the bed in her hospital room, anxious to be free of this prison. She was grateful for the clothes Heidi Callahan—her half sister—had purchased for her. Only a few years older than Sylvie, Heidi sat across from her in the only chair in the room. Her rich and thick chocolate hair splayed across and down her shoulders. Both the hair and the deep warmth in her smile reminded Sylvie of Cade. She was so beautiful. Sylvie wondered why she hadn't inherited some of those looks, but that was the least of her concerns.

Still, she could see some resemblance between them.

Sylvie had mixed emotions about this whole thing. "I wish we could have met under different circumstances."

"Whatever the circumstances, at least we've met, and at least you are alive." Heidi pushed from the chair, her five-month pregnancy barely showing. She was pregnant with the niece that Cade had mentioned. "I'm looking forward to spending some time together when this is all over."

"Yes, when this is all over." Sylvie knew her own smile was tenuous, at best.

"I have an appointment with my OB soon but I'm going to use the little girl's room before I leave. Not like I didn't just go. Just wait until you get pregnant." Heidi gave a bashful grin then disappeared.

At her words, Sylvie could hardly hold back her tears, and let them fall when Heidi was gone.

The fact that Heidi was pregnant drove home Sylvie's misgivings about the trouble she was facing—she hadn't known her search for answers would put others in danger. Nor had she known she would meet her half siblings like this—and had been completely unprepared in that respect. They'd all stopped in the day after Cade's appearance. He'd given her a day and not one minute more to prepare for meeting the rest of the family. That meeting had all but overwhelmed her on top of another attempt on her life.

They'd all crowded into the room to see her. First, Heidi and her husband, Isaiah, then Cade's wife, Leah, who had presented her and Cade's son, little Scottie. Then firefighter David and his wife, Tracy, who had newborn twin boys; and Adam and Cobie, who'd recently gotten married. What a wonderful, beautiful family, and if Sylvie had any regrets, it was that she had missed out on knowing them all this time, and on knowing her real father.

Would that have been so bad? Having time to know him? To know them all? She couldn't help but think he would have wanted to know her, too. But she'd been informed he hadn't been aware of her existence. And what about her grandfather? Had Regina even told *him* about her? Tears burned her eyes, mingling with the anger of it.

Mom, why? Why didn't you tell him? Why did you keep me a secret until it was too late?

She wiped away the tears. She couldn't complain about her childhood. She'd had a good one. The man she'd known as her father, the man her mother had married, had been good to her. Had loved her, though he'd never adopted Sylvie. She'd grown up using his last name, regardless, and had taken it as her own.

Maybe her mother had wanted to keep a legal tie back to Scott Warren, Sylvie's real father. But she had a feeling her mother had prevented Damon from legally adopting Sylvie because even though he'd been a good father, he'd been an awful husband. Yet she'd stayed with him.

Sylvie didn't know the reasons.

All she knew was that she was torn between trusting the man she'd loved as a child, and nursing her bitterness over the betrayal she'd learned about as a teen. And the fear she'd heard in her mother's voice. How could he treat her mother one way and Sylvie another?

She was relieved he didn't know she was in the hospital and wasn't here. How sad was that?

But she couldn't trust Damon Masters, the man who'd been a father to her. He manipulated people for his own purposes. She'd trusted her mother, although the woman had kept secrets. Secrets like what she planned to do in Mountain Cove that would "shake things up." Secrets that Sylvie believed led to her death.

The search for answers had now turned treacherous.

There was only one good thing to come of it and that was meeting her family—the whole bunch of them. Was this the only way she ever would have met them? Forced into it by circumstances?

Didn't matter anymore. She was in a situation that required her full attention.

Sylvie fiddled with the splash caddy that had protected her driver's license and bank card, secured against her body while in the water. The troopers said her boat hadn't been recovered, and she'd reported it stolen to the insurance company. Other than the rotating officers guarding her room, the police hadn't been back since their initial questioning. She had no idea if they would search the area where she'd found what might have been part of the missing aircraft, but they were definitely searching for the man who'd tried to kill her twice now. Once in the water and then in the hospital. Regardless, Sylvie believed she was on her own in finding out the truth.

Heidi returned from the little girl's room, as she called it. "Billy should be here soon. Do you want me to wait with you?"

"Billy? You mean Will?"

Heidi angled her head, a curious smile playing on her lips. "I guess so."

Sylvie shook her head. "No, no. Please, go to your appointment. I'll be fine."

"Okay, then, I'll head out—but there's something I want to say first. Growing up with three brothers, I always prayed for a sister. Then I got three sisters-in-law, Leah, Tracy and Cobie, and now you, a half sibling. I just wish we could have known each other growing up." Heidi's face colored.

Now that would have been awkward. She suspected Heidi thought the same thing. Sylvie was still baffled at how graciously the family had received her—the child their father had created while cheating on their mother. Learning of his betrayal, even as adults, had to leave them confused and bitter. Would they have been able to handle it as children? She wasn't sure. But she did know that her life would have been richer and fuller for all these years if her siblings had been part of it all along.

"Yeah, me, too." Sylvie had been on the outside of the family looking in until this week, when she'd entered the hospital fighting for her life.

Will stepped into the room and relief whooshed through Sylvie. She wasn't exactly sure why.

"Well," Heidi said, "I should get going. I want to head Isaiah off at the entrance. He's being so wonderful—overprotective, but wonderful. See you guys later." Heidi waved and stepped out.

Will turned his attention to Sylvie, his brown eyes

cocooning her in warmth and safety. She tried to shake it off. The effect he had on her scared her. She needed distance. Especially since being near her had put him directly in harm's way too many times already.

How did she remedy that?

Will was all she had in this. The only person she could trust. She'd never needed anyone before. Didn't want to need him now. Was it really necessary to depend on him? Surely now that law enforcement was involved, she'd be able to get through this on her own.

He sat in the chair. "I'm sorry I'm late. Have you signed the release papers yet?"

"Yes, I'm waiting on the nurse to bring the wheelchair, which is so stupid."

"Hospital policy."

"Yeah, I get that." Sylvie needed to say goodbye. She needed time to regroup and figure this out alone. Not put him in danger anymore.

He'd argue, of course. They were on the same search, after all. But Sylvie wasn't at all sure that she wanted him to find the answers. She was afraid of what that truth was, and she couldn't trust Will with secrets.

He'd already shown her that.

Sylvie shifted, uncomfortable with her thoughts. Her need to get away had as much to do with the warmth she felt—the increase in her pulse at his intense gaze—as it did the need to keep him out of danger, and perhaps to keep him from learning things she'd rather keep hidden.

What was he thinking, just now?

He'd quickly flown right over the barriers she'd erected to protect her heart. How could that happen when Sylvie knew better than to let her guard down?

Her mother's life had practically self-destructed over two different men she'd loved.

She let thoughts of the way her real father had hurt her mother wash over her. Images of how Damon had treated her mother accosted her. Those thoughts should do the trick. Help her cut Will loose.

"What's wrong?" His brows twisted. "Sylvie, tell me."

"I don't know what you're doing here. You didn't have to come."

He stood, startling her. "What do you mean? Of course you know why I'm here. Have you forgotten we're in this together? Someone is trying to kill you, tried to kill both of us, and our mothers died together. Sylvie, this involves us both."

She averted her gaze, hating the pain she was causing him.

"Sylvie, look at me."

She didn't want to. "Will, I'm going home. I'll take a cab to the airport and be back in Seattle in a few hours."

"Are you forgetting that someone found you scuba diving in the middle of nowhere? That someone followed us both to Snake's cabin and shot down the man who rescued us? And someone came into this hospital and tried to kill you here. Are you forgetting that?"

Sylvie hated how weak she still felt, but she sprung to her feet to meet Will's challenge. "No, Will, I haven't forgotten. But I cannot be responsible for anyone else getting killed in the crossfire. No one has tried to kill you, except as a way to get to me. Even yesterday, the man with the gun—he only aimed it at me. Your life was at risk merely from your proximity to me. Now, argue with me on that point."

The nurse came in with the wheelchair and cocked a brow. "Keep it down in here." She gave Sylvie a cursory glance. "You ready?"

Nodding, Sylvie sat in the wheelchair.

The nurse pushed her forward, and she felt all the more an idiot—getting scolded for yelling like she was a misbehaving child. Stupid hospital policy. She wanted to tell Will to go home, but she wouldn't make more of a scene in the hospital. Wouldn't embarrass him.

"You hate flying, Sylvie." He walked next to her as the nurse pushed the wheelchair.

"What?"

"You're not going to fly back to Seattle because you hate flying, remember?"

Sylvie refused to continue this conversation until they had privacy. Thankfully, Will didn't press her for an immediate answer. The nurse pushed the wheelchair onto the elevator. They rode the box down to the next floor. The wheelchair rolled forward until Sylvie was finally wheeled through the hospital exit. She stood and bid the nurse to take the wheelchair and go. Sylvie wished she had called for her own cab, but Heidi had interrupted her with the clothes for which she was grateful. And then Will turned up to escort her.

So she couldn't escape right away. But at least now she could reply to Will. "I remember."

His eyes were devoid of their usual warmth. "Then you'll remember that my mother also died on that plane. I'm in up to my neck. I can't keep you here. I can't even force you to work with me on this, but I'll ask you to do me one favor."

"What's that?"

"Tell Chief Winters everything you know, so that we can work on things from Mountain Cove."

Mountain Cove.

Sylvie blew out a breath. She hadn't exactly told them everything. She hadn't mentioned her suspicions about Damon because she had nothing to go on, no specific proof to inplicate him, nor had they asked. But Sylvie'd heard the fear in her mother's voice, and she was still trying to figure out why her mother was running to Mountain Cove, of all places.

Once again, Will waited for her reply. Sylvie watched patients being wheeled from the hospital and greeted by loved ones. Others entering the facility. She thought again of her mother's last words. The voice mail she'd left.

Sylvie, it's Mom. I can't say much over the phone but please be careful. Hesitation, then a whisper, *Watch your back, baby. Be aware of your surroundings. I'll explain why tomorrow. I'm flying to Mountain Cove on a bush plane. I know what you're thinking, but I'll tell you more when I get there. It's Damon... Oh... I've gotta go now, but I wanted you to know just in case... well, that I love you...*

Just in case what? That her plane crashed? At first, she actually thought Mom had been reminding Sylvie to be careful while scuba diving.

But to Mountain Cove? That meant all kinds of trouble.

The way she'd said *I love you* like it might be her last time, and the fearful tone in her voice, and Sylvie knew her message had layers of meaning. That she was scared. She'd brought up Damon. What had she been going to say? Was she finally trying to leave him?

And now she was dead.

Sylvie decided she should try to contact Ashley Wilson as soon as she made it back to Seattle. Her mother and Ashley, Damon's assistant, were friends. Sylvie had joined them for lunch on occasion. Ashley might know something that Regina had failed to share with Sylvie.

But whatever Ashley might say, Sylvie could only think of one reason her mother would return to Mountain Cove.

She was running from Damon.

He would never believe she had gone there, since he knew about her bad memories of the town. It was the only place she could escape him.

Sylvie couldn't forget that Damon was not only her stepfather, but he was also a powerful man. And apparently more dangerous than she could have imagined. Nausea roiled at the thought.

A chill ran over Sylvie. She glanced at Will, who still waited for her reply. She had to admit the man was patient.

"I've already talked to the Alaska State Troopers. I don't have time to go to Mountain Cove. My vacation time is up in a week."

"No need to go to Mountain Cove to talk to Chief Winters." Will gestured behind Sylvie.

She turned and a man stepped forward from where he leaned against a column. Though he wasn't dressed in uniform, she glanced back at Will. "Chief Winters?"

TEN

Will ushered Sylvie into the taxi that he'd called, and Chief Winters flanked her on the other side.

Inside the cab Sylvie's wide, questioning eyes trapped him. "What was that about?"

"I was afraid the attackers might not let you walk away from the hospital without trying something else. I asked Chief Winters to come today as a favor, to make sure you were able to leave safely."

Will wished they could have had a big security detail of Juneau Police or Alaska State Troopers, but Sylvie's troubles didn't rank, and all he could get was Chief Winters. This wasn't even the man's jurisdiction. The Alaska State Troopers were looking into Snake's murder and investigating Sylvie's story. They worked off facts, and Will and Sylvie didn't have many to offer. Add to that Alaska was one-fifth the size of the lower forty-eight. The geography and remoteness presented barriers.

"Thanks, but…" She lifted fiery eyes to him, defiance burning in them. "I can't live in hiding. I'm not going to hire a bodyguard to go with me everywhere."

Now, there's an idea. Something Will could have grinned about if this wasn't serious.

Sure, he had a business to run, but he'd put it on hold until he resolved this. He had two planes to recoup and needed to discover the truth about what happened to his mother before he'd open up for business again. In the meantime, he referred his business to other bush pilot friends and hoped his regulars would come back when this was over.

"First things first." Chief Winters rubbed his ear. "Let's get some coffee. Grab some lunch. I'm starved. And you can tell me your story while we eat."

Sylvie gave Will a look. She didn't want to repeat herself. He understood, but he kept silent until they made it to their destination.

They entered the coffee shop a few streets over from the hospital. Chief Winters chose a booth in the far corner, his back to the wall. Of course. Following his lead, Will sat next to him, regretting his move when Sylvie slid in across from them. He hoped she didn't feel as if she was under interrogation, with them ganged up against her. She eyed their surroundings, and Will did, too. A couple of older men at a table. A young mother coddling an infant and toddler with Cheerios while she waited for someone. The door chimed when another man entered and searched for a seat.

Was he someone following them? Someone bent on silencing Sylvie? Will continued to watch the man, while the waitress approached their booth and took their orders.

Will waited until she'd returned with their beverages then said to the chief, "Thanks again for agreeing to meet us."

"Your mother was a friend, you know that." Chief

Winters sugared up his coffee. "I want to keep my finger on the pulse of this investigation."

He glanced at Sylvie, who sipped iced tea and looked like a caged animal watching for an escape. So far, she hadn't said a word since they'd left the cab. He'd hoped she would feel more comfortable with Chief Winters than with the Alaska State Troopers who had interrogated them both.

"I'm glad you're out of the hospital," Will said. "I can't think of a less safe environment for you, confined to a bed like that, even with the security detail stationed at your door. I noticed he was conveniently gone today."

"They're spread too thin, Will, just as we all are." The police chief shifted his gaze to Sylvie. "So, tell me about yourself."

Will leaned against the seat back. With his easy ways, Chief Winters was good at getting people to talk, and Will was counting on that. But after half an hour, Will knew nothing more about things than he had before. At least Chief Winters heard her story, and Will could trust the man to stay in touch with his Alaska State Troopers counterparts regarding the investigation, if it went anywhere.

Sylvie pushed her emptied plate forward. "Thanks for the meal. Much better than hospital food. And, Will—" appreciation poured from her hazel eyes, but it was mingled with regret "—I know you want answers to what happened to your mother as much as I want them for myself, but there's nothing else I can do here. I need to get home and regroup. Figure things out from there, if I can."

"This is about more than getting answers." Will couldn't say why he did it, but he reached across the

table and grabbed her hand, which put a different meaning on his words than he'd intended. "This is about
keeping you safe. Someone's trying to kill you, Sylvie."

Her lips curved into a soft smile. "You're my hero,
Will. But…"

"I'm not looking to be a hero. I wasn't waiting to
hear you tell me that. I want to know how you're going
to stay alive. What's your plan?"

"I think… I hope all this was just a warning. If I go
back home then it should stop."

Will removed his hand from hers. She was too smart
to believe that. What was she trying to pull? Will
wouldn't let her try to fool him. "Don't do this. Don't
treat me like an idiot."

"Excuse me?"

"You're too smart to believe it was only a warning.
I know that. *You* know that."

Sylvie looked to Chief Winters for help. Will kind
of wanted his help, too, in convincing her she couldn't
do this alone. Wisely, Chief Winters chose to say nothing at all.

"Okay, so you got me." She fidgeted with her paper
napkin. "But it doesn't matter. I'm leaving today. I have
to go home. Look what happened to your plane because
of me. Look what happened to Snake! I won't be the reason something even worse happens to you, Will. Now,
gentlemen, if you'll excuse me, I'm leaving."

Sylvie slid from the booth and started for the door.
Will moved to follow her but Chief Winters grabbed
him, held him captive. "Let her go for now."

"But…"

"It's clear she needs space. We can't force her to stay."

"You agreed to be here when she left the hospital in

case these men tried something else, and now we're just going to let her go? Shouldn't we watch out for her?"

"We can't follow her to Seattle."

They watched through the window as Sylvie climbed into a taxi, vulnerable, defenseless.

"Maybe you can't follow her, but I can."

Amusement flashed in Chief Winters's gaze. "I'm getting the sense that this is about a lot more than a murder investigation for you. More than just keeping her safe."

The man's words hit him in the gut. "I'm not interested in her, if that's what you mean. I'm only interested in protecting her and finding out who had the motivation and ability to knock a plane out of the sky. Who is trying to kill her."

"A noble cause, to be sure." Chief Winters stretched his legs beneath the booth. "But looks like Sylvie isn't the only one who hasn't realized the truth."

Will hoped Chief Winters wasn't reading too much into his reaction. He didn't want to accept that he was growing more attached to Sylvie every day. But the police chief, trained to read people, hadn't been fooled. Will had been the only fool. He had some kind of thing for Sylvie Masters. How did he cut off those feelings and protect her at the same time?

Will stood and dropped a few small bills on the table. Enough to pay for their meals and a tip.

"Better hurry if you're going to catch her," Chief Winters said. "Don't worry about me, I can find my own way home. Let me know what you learn, if anything. I'll do the same. And Will, be careful. Don't let your attraction to her cloud your judgment. These people play for keeps."

*   *   *

Sylvie stood on the ferry that would deliver her to
Bellingham, Washington. If she'd flown, it would have
taken a few hours. By boat, it would take two and a half
days to get there.

Nausea roiled inside. What was she doing here on
this ferry filled with strangers? The boat was packed
with fishermen, those seeking work or adventure, retired couples and a few that looked like they were up
to no good.

The ferry from Bellingham to southeast Alaska was
commonly termed "the poor man's cruise." She'd been
fortunate to book passage, but she'd been too late to get
a cabin. Nor had she had the foresight to bring a small
tent like so many others who would sleep out on the
deck and under the solarium.

She'd have to join the ranks of those sleeping on the
chairs. At least she could rent a pillow and blanket. If
only she'd gotten over her ridiculous fear of flying, but
her experience with Will had only served to deepen
her fears. That, and the fact her mother had died in a
plane crash.

So she couldn't bring herself to book a flight from
Juneau to Seattle.

Supposedly, flying was the safest way to travel. But
Sylvie had never been one to count the stats. Standing
outside, the wind blew cold and continuously with the
movement of the ship. She tugged her hood over her
head. Drew in a breath of fresh Alaskan air. Took in
the view. Gray clouds hung low, sometimes hiding the
peaks of snow-capped mountains. Tree-laden islands,
some surprisingly small and others massive by contrast,

dotted the channel of the Inside Passage. The scenery brought a measure of peace.

And at least for the time being, Sylvie felt safe from killers. After all, how could the men looking for her have known she'd choose this route to get home? If they were looking for her, surely they'd be looking at airports.

This hadn't been such a bad idea, after all. She needed time to think about everything that had happened without nurses hovering or interrupting her thoughts every couple of hours, and without Will's hospital visits. Now that she had been released, she was free. She could put distance between them and keep him from harm's way.

Why had he come to see her so often and stayed so long every time he came to the hospital? He said it was because they were in this together because of their mothers. But the tenderness in his touch and the care pouring from his eyes told her it was more than that. He was there because he believed there was something more personal between him and Sylvie.

Was he right? She wasn't sure. His presence scrambled her thoughts. She liked him, and she didn't want to like him. She owed him her life, and she didn't want to owe anyone. Sylvie couldn't lead him on like that. Couldn't hurt him, couldn't hurt herself, letting something develop between them that could go nowhere.

But despite her persuasive arguments to leave Will behind, she knew she could use someone's help right now, which had her wishing she hadn't pushed him away. Make that run away. And that was what Sylvie had done. She'd run away from Will.

Leaning over the banister, she watched the ferry's wake. As a diving trainer, she understood the importance of being smart and planning out her actions down to the minute. Anything else could get her killed. And yet she'd almost lost her life due to her gross miscalculations. How could she protect herself now? Backing off seemed the most obvious answer, but it was one she wouldn't accept.

Regardless of her mistakes, she would keep searching for the truth that someone didn't want her to find.

A shiver crawled over her. She turned her back to the beauty of southeast Alaska to watch other passengers, wondering if she might actually be in danger from any of them.

Were her attackers still after her? Would they follow her back to Washington or wait for her there?

And the biggest question of all. Who was *they*?

A gust whipped across her face, raking her eyes. Sylvie blinked to moisten them.

Was Damon involved? Had he killed her mother? Her heart ached at the thought. She couldn't accept that he might be the reason her mother was dead. Couldn't be behind those who had tried to kill her. Even though their relationship had been strained these past few years, and even though he was an adulterer, Sylvie found it hard to believe Damon could be capable of murder. Could she trust him? No. And he certainly had the means.

She wished she could think of someone else who might be responsible, but she couldn't.

Across the channel, she watched a cruise ship make its way north. Sylvie blinked up in time to see a man standing on the other side of the ferry. His gaze flicked away from her. Had he been watching her? He disappeared around a corner.

Dread coiled around her spine.

She was definitely in over her head. If someone had followed her, intending to kill her or push her over the side, how could she protect herself? How did she stay alive long enough to solve this—something her mother hadn't been able to do? If only Will was here. If she'd asked him, he would have come.

Stop it! Stop thinking about him. What was done, was done. Sylvie was on her own now, as it should be.

Thinking back on their last conversation, she decided that a bodyguard wasn't such a bad idea, at least until this was over. Normally this would be something for which she would ask for her stepfather's assistance. He had his own security detail. But she couldn't trust them now—not while she suspected he might be involved. Sylvie hated the tumultuous thoughts coursing through her. He'd given her a good home, everything she'd wanted except for two parents who loved each other. What had her mother running to Mountain Cove if not her husband? She was always on a witch hunt; what had she discovered? Whatever it was had gotten her killed.

Suddenly, the wide open space, the waters of the channel and the forest, closed in on Sylvie. The air smothered her. When she glanced around, she realized that she was alone on this portion of the deck. Where had everyone gone? The cafeteria for a hot meal?

She had to get out of here, but she was stuck on this ferry for three days.

Three days.

Her pulse shot up as Sylvie pushed from the rail to run, to flee. To where, she had no idea.

She hurried around a corner and ran into a wall of a man. A yelp escaped as the man gripped her. Her heart jumped to her throat and she tried to free herself, except his grip tightened as he pulled her close.

Familiar brown eyes stared back. "Sylvie."

"Will?" Relief rippled through her.

"Yes, I'm here. What's wrong?" He slowly released his grip, his concerned gaze roaming her face then scrutinizing their surroundings.

"What…what are you doing here?" She hadn't meant to sound so harsh, but anger battled with her sheer joy at seeing him.

"You don't seem glad to see me." His brow quirked.

Her jumbled emotions kept her from a coherent response, then finally, "Why are you just now letting me know you were here? I…" Yeah, she was glad to see him, but she wouldn't let him know how much. She was more than angry he'd been following her against her wishes.

"I wanted to make sure you were safe. But I wasn't sure about your reaction when you found out." He glanced off in the distance. "I was working up my nerve to approach you, but then you disappeared."

"Will…" She managed a shallow gasp of his name. Pressed her forehead against his chest like an idiot. He would see right through her if she didn't pull herself together. "I had a feeling I was being followed. If only I had known it was you."

"I could have misjudged the situation. Are you saying I shouldn't have come?"

Oh, now he was teasing her. Of course he could tell

that she was glad to see him. Her reaction said everything, more than she wanted to reveal. But she wouldn't say the words to him. Tell him that she liked that he'd come after her, that he'd followed. That he wanted to protect her.

"Will, I'll ask again, why are you here?" She wanted to hear all those things from him.

"I wanted to protect you. I was scared for you when you left, so I followed. I would think that was obvious, after everything we've been through. After I already told you that we're in this together. And after…" Will's attention snagged on something behind her. "Looks like someone besides me followed you, and he's coming this way."

ELEVEN

Will shoved Sylvie behind him and faced the man who strode toward them. This part of the deck was empty of others who might interfere at the moment. Could be the man had nothing to do with Sylvie, and Will was acting the fool—but he wasn't going to take that chance.

The man, wearing a dark navy jacket, had the broad chest and thick neck of a marine. The stride of someone who never lost a battle. He watched the mountains beyond them as though interested in the scenery, except his eyes flicked to Sylvie. One time. That was all it took to telegraph his intentions. A tall, skinny woman strolled along the railing with a video camera, heading their way. If the man was going to strike, it would be now, before anyone else approached and got in the way.

Sylvie tugged at him, tried coming around from behind him. He knew she didn't want him to get hurt, but Will stood his ground, protecting her if the man was bent on harm. As he closed in on them, strolling along as if he was simply riding the ferry back to Washington, Will braced himself for what was to come. The truth was always there in the eyes, just like it was in this man's eyes now. This wasn't the guy from the hospital, but he read the man's intentions all the same—his sheer determination to kill Sylvie.

This scene had become all too familiar.

"Will." Sylvie fought him now, making his task more difficult. "This is why I wanted to leave you!"

The man approached quickly, lifting his arm from beneath his jacket, leaving Will only a millisecond to respond. He lunged, forcing the man's weapon-wielding hand down. A bullet fired off, hitting the water to the left. Screams erupted from elsewhere on the ferry. The woman with the camera began shouting for others to come and assist, while she filmed the whole thing.

Who was Sylvie that someone would risk killing her on a ferry in the middle of the water, leaving the attacker no escape, nowhere to run? Her killers were becoming more desperate.

Will's muscles strained as he held the man off. He grunted with the effort. "Who. *Are*. You? What do you want?"

If Will could hold the man in this position long enough, the ferry security guard would arrive and detain him. They could get to the bottom of this, but the man broke free. Will landed a punch square to his jaw. The weapon dropped to the water.

To Will's astonishment, the attacker climbed over the rail and jumped into the cold waters of the channel, a good drop from the deck of the ferry.

Will wanted to follow him. Sylvie grabbed him. "Will, no! Are you crazy?"

Adrenaline coursed through him as he started over, determined to swim after the man and beat the truth from him. End this for Sylvie. Men flanked him and pulled him back. One of them was a security guard.

They all watched in silence as the guilty party swam away. In the distance, a boat appeared. Was that the same boat that had been waiting where Sylvie had been attacked beneath the water?

"Aren't you going to do something?" Will asked the guard. "Follow him?" Will leaned over his thighs to catch his breath, his ribs throbbing. He hadn't remembered being jabbed there.

"We'll call the Coast Guard."

"I taped the whole thing," the woman with the camera said. "You can see if you can identify him."

The security guard thanked her.

Will pushed himself upright and looked into Sylvie's tormented eyes. "Are you okay?"

"Me? I'm fine. You're the one who's hurt. Why do you keep doing this? Showing up and standing between me and the bad guys?"

He would have expected gratitude, but all he saw in her eyes was anger. "And what if I hadn't been here? What if I hadn't come this time? Where would you be? Could you have fought that guy?"

"I don't want anyone else to get hurt because of me, but you're right, Will. I can't do this alone."

The security guard escorted Will and Sylvie to a room where a nurse saw to Will's injuries—a bruised rib, she determined—and the security officer, a retired police officer out of Sitka, questioned them. Sylvie explained that the Alaska State Troopers were investigating, and would need to be informed of the latest incident. At least the woman had documented what happened for them.

When they were left alone in the sparse and economical office, Will watched Sylvie stare out the window and hug herself. Her hazel eyes had lost their shimmer. That cut him to the bone.

"Did you recognize that guy?" he asked.

"No. Like I told the police, and you and Chief Winters, the guy in the hospital, he was the diver who came at me. I only saw his eyes behind his mask, but I could never forget them. But this guy, nope. If I had recognized him, I would have gone for help immediately once I saw him."

"So Diverman was at the hospital, and maybe this guy was Rifleman, the man who was on the island and shot at you and my plane. We need to see if the police will put you in a safe house until they resolve this."

She gave a scoffing laugh. "Which police, Will? The jurisdiction is all over the place. Besides, I think this originated outside Alaska, and I'm heading back to Seattle. I can talk to someone there."

"I've always had the feeling you knew more than you were saying, Sylvie. Now would be a good time to tell me what you do know. Tell me everything."

Sylvie flinched but didn't answer. She liked to think before she responded. He'd give her a few moments. Ignoring the pain in his ribs, Will shoved to his feet and approached. From behind her, he watched out the window, as well. Everything looked so gray and hopeless. He fought the urge to wrap his arms around her, hold her, chase the darkness away. He wouldn't get the answers he wanted, couldn't hang around long enough to protect her, if he scared her away by trying to force her to comply. Force her to answer.

Will couldn't help himself and lifted his hand. Indecision kept it hovering above her shoulder, then finally, he let it drop on the soft threads of her navy fleece hoodie. She tensed then relaxed. He thought she might even lean into him as she'd done on the deck when he'd first revealed himself.

She exhaled and slowly turned. Facing him, she was much too close. He let his gaze take in the face he had once thought not quite pretty, but he'd changed his mind so quickly. Once he got to know her and saw her inner strength—that light shining from within that poured from her eyes and her smile—she became the most beautiful woman he'd ever seen.

He'd let his hand drop from her shoulder, but now both hands rubbed her arms. More reassurance? He wasn't sure, but his hands had a mind of their own, and he let them. He was rewarded when he coaxed the smallest of smiles into her drawn face.

"I'll tell you everything I know, Will. I'm sorry. I should have trusted you completely. It seemed too private, too personal, and I wasn't sure about any of it. Wasn't sure I wanted to share my family secrets. But now I know what I want to do, and where I want to go."

"I'm listening."

"I want to go home. To my mother's home where she lived with Damon, my stepfather. The house where I grew up. In my last conversation with her, she was running scared. She called to warn me to *watch my back*, and said she would tell me more when she got to Mountain Cove. Then she told me that she loved me. Something in her tone made it sound like she was telling me in case she never got the chance to say it again."

"Do you have any idea who might have scared her that badly?" Will asked gently.

"My stepfather. Damon cheated on my mother," she replied. "A lot. I don't understand why she didn't just leave, but he had power over her to keep her. I think she was scared of him, too. She brought up his name in her voice mail but didn't finish what she was going to say. Regardless, it seems she finally freed herself or got the courage to leave. But that's why she went to Mountain Cove. He would never think to follow her there in a million years. And she would never go there except to get away from him."

Sylvie pressed her face into her hands.

Will gave her time to compose herself.

She dropped her hands and moved to sit in the chair. "As soon as I heard that she had died in a plane crash, I listened to her message again. Then I heard it for what it was. She was running scared. Tried to warn me. I knew I had to find that plane so that I could know if someone had murdered her."

"Then men showed up to silence you."

"And I knew then. I mean, you and I were running scared and it took me some time to come to grips with it, but deep down, I knew."

"How did you find out about the plane crash, her death, if your mother was able to keep her whereabouts a secret from your stepfather? Who knew she'd gotten on that plane? Even I didn't know. She was the surprise package. My mother made her living delivering unscheduled passengers and surprises to the bush."

Sylvie stared at him, unblinking. "Damon, my stepfather. He called to tell me the news. He knew where she was, after all." She contemplated the words. "Will... he's a powerful man. He could afford to pay someone to sabotage the plane. He could afford to send people after me."

"But you don't want to believe it."

"No, even after everything, I don't want to believe it. And that's why I have to go home. I need to find the truth. She had to have left something. Maybe I can prove that Damon wasn't involved."

"Let me get this straight. You're saying you suspect your stepfather could have something to do with the plane crash. That he killed your mother and now you want to go see him. You want to go right into the lion's den?" Will couldn't help his incredulous tone. "Sylvie, why haven't you told this to the police, if you suspect the man?"

"I have nothing concrete. I don't want it to be true. I don't want all the ugliness that happened between them to have resulted in her murder. I want to prove my suspicions wrong. But I think I could find some answers if I look through Mom's things. After the memorial service I couldn't face going through them as if she was gone, never to return. I think that's another reason why I wanted to find the plane first—because that was the only thing that could make it real."

He understood that all too well, and it was what had thrown their lives together. "I don't think you should go see him."

"I'm not going to see him. He won't even be there."

"I don't understand why you didn't share this information. If he's guilty, the police could have resolved this by now."

She shook her head. "No, he's powerful. They wouldn't investigate him without a reason."

Who was this man? What did he do for a living? What was Will missing here? Questions stumbled around in the back of Will's mind, but he wouldn't interrupt.

"He loved my mother in his own way, but like I told you he cheated on her." She glanced at Will. "Don't say anything, okay? Believe me, my mother tortured herself with the guilt over what she'd done in Mountain Cove and felt like it had all come back on her. She'd committed adultery with a married man, now it was her turn."

"I'm not judging anyone, Sylvie."

"On the surface he was good to the both of us. A wonderful father to me. There wasn't anything I wanted that he didn't give except for more time with him. But there was another side to him, which made him seem cruel and manipulative. He hid that from me as much as he could, but I still caught flashes of it—and I think my mother saw more. He knows how to be very persuasive and has kept my mother by his side even with his ongoing affairs. On the one hand I love him, and on the other I hate him for how he treated her. The betrayal. I heard the arguments down the hall, or my mother's tears after phone calls. I cried myself to sleep at night. And between my two fathers, and how they treated my mother, I never wanted to be in a relationship myself." She'd rushed the last words, as if she hadn't meant to say them. "But that's beside the point."

Will heard her loud and clear. She'd dropped that little hint to make sure he understood there could be nothing between them. Fine with him—he had his own reasons for avoiding relationships. "I don't think it's safe to go to his home even if he won't be there. He sounds like a dangerous man."

"You don't understand. He doted on me. Made me feel like a little princess. That's why I'm so torn. I can't imagine that he would ever harm me. In fact, he taught me to be strong and independent, and to find my own way, which is exactly what I did. I pursued a career in the thing I loved most—scuba diving. So I can't—I won't—point the finger at him if I don't have to. I need to find proof that he isn't involved. In finding that truth, I'll find out what happened to my mother. Who killed her and who is trying to kill me."

"And you can't think of anyone else who would want to harm your mother?" Or his. Will didn't put much stock in someone trying to kill his mother when all the focus seemed to be on Sylvie and her almost discovering the plane.

"I wish… I wish I could. Can you imagine if I accused him to the police, what that would do to him if it wasn't true? And that's if I could even get the police to take the idea seriously. No, I need to find out for myself." Sylvie dropped her face into her hands. "I've never been in so much pain."

He didn't like seeing her hurting. Nor did he like her plan. Sylvie could be right that the evidence they'd find would exonerate her stepfather. Or she could be so completely blinded by her need for a loving father figure—considering she had two fails on that point— that she wasn't willing to face the truth.

He couldn't stop himself this time and reached for her, tugged her close and wrapped his arms around her. He was surprised she came into them so quickly and molded against him willingly. It felt right. He wanted to hold her for the sake of holding her, in spite of their mutual determination to avoid relationships.

"You need to realize that your safety is more important than finding out the truth."

Sylvie was becoming more important to him personally than anything else.

And that thought scared him to death. That truth was more dangerous than anything he'd faced so far. But he had the feeling that she'd started something that would never stop, even if she quit searching. It wouldn't end well for Sylvie, for either of them, unless they uncovered the truth and exposed the killers.

God, please don't let it be her stepfather. That would crush her. But what other possibilities were there? He'd see this through with her until it was over. Then, in order to protect his heart, in order to survive, Will Pierson would say goodbye to Sylvie.

It was all about survival of the fittest.

TWELVE

The ferry to Washington had been the longest three days of her life, and though Will had tried to convince her to get off in Ketchikan where he could get them a seaplane ride into Washington and shorten their trip, she had refused. So they slept under the solarium in the deck chairs with the rest of the ferry crowd who hadn't brought tents or rented cabins.

She'd never met anyone like him. Somehow through all this she had to keep her distance emotionally. And given that she'd just spent almost three days with him putting aside thoughts of the danger chasing them, and instead enjoying the sites of southeast Alaska—even getting a chance to watch the whales—like it was some sort of vacation, keeping her distance emotionally was becoming harder every day. Still, she wouldn't have had it any other way. He'd kept her company and he'd kept her alive.

So far.

But it would all come to an end soon.

She and Will expected her pursuers to be watching and awaiting their arrival in Washington.

Once the ferry docked at the terminal in Bellingham,

Will rented a car for them at the Avis counter while she hung back against the wall, watching the crowd for any familiar faces. Her car was still parked at the marina from which she'd taken her boat up through the Inside Passage on her own. Had it really been more than a week ago? Will insisted she leave her car sitting and let him do the renting so they wouldn't leave any unnecessary trails, credit card or otherwise.

When he finished at the counter he had a big dimpled grin when he found her, and then he led her out the door and to the parking lot of rental cars. They passed by every one of the midsized sedans. Practical and economical. Then stopped at a cherry-red Chevrolet Camaro SS.

"Seriously, Will?"

"This has a V8. We need something with a powerful engine. I don't want to be stuck in a Prius if I need to lose someone. Besides, they were all out of BMWs." He opened the door for her, his smile fading as his gaze took in the parking lot and others climbing into the more practical midsized cars. She scanned the crowd, as well, and saw no sign of the man who'd attacked her at the hospital or the one from the ferry.

So far, so good.

When he looked down at her sitting in the sports car, the grin came back again as he shut the door. He dropped into the seat on the driver's side.

"Are you sure this isn't just your way of living out some unrealized juvenile dream?" She hoped he caught her teasing tone.

"I live my dream every time I climb into a bush plane." He started the ignition and paused to listen to the engine purr. "But if I can't fly, this will do in a pinch."

Looking out the window, watching for their pursuers, Sylvie smiled as Will steered them from the parking lot. This guy might be a lot of fun in a world where she wasn't being pursued by killers. But Sylvie shoved those thoughts out of her mind.

They stopped at a strip mall where she and Will bought a few additional items of clothing and grabbed some lunch. Better to buy new clothes and avoid going back to her apartment where dangerous men could be waiting to kill her, until this was over.

She had one destination in mind, and that was her stepfather's mansion, where she'd grown up. The last place her mother had been before her tragic death. Although the killers had found Sylvie in the waters of the channel, in Snake's cabin, in the hospital and on the ferry, she could hope they wouldn't follow her to her stepfather's home. If the worst-case scenario was true, and he was involved, he would never allow anything to happen at the refurbished historical mansion he'd purchased for her mother as a wedding gift.

A morbid way of believing she would be safe there. All things considered, though, it was as safe a place as any.

At least he wouldn't be there this week, and Sylvie could search Mom's things without having to face him. He was the head of an international corporation and traveled often, and Sylvie knew he was in Asia for a month. He hated the house, and she figured he would move out and into another monstrosity as soon as was socially acceptable given the loss of his wife. With all the doubt and suspicion coursing through her, she didn't think she could look him in the eyes. If she saw him now, in her current frame of mind, she might accuse him to his face just to see his reaction. But he could be convincing, even if he was guilty, which meant she had to find solid evidence—something only she could get her hands on.

Would she be strong enough to see through him if it came to that?

God, please don't let him be involved in her death...

She didn't think anything could hurt worse than his betrayal of their loving, happy family, but a murder would certainly slice her heart in two.

Her thoughts were jumbled as each passing mile put her closer to home. She thought about what she would say to the housekeeping staff when she arrived. Though the house had been Sylvie's home, too—her bedroom was still the same and she was always welcome—she wouldn't give her usual courtesy call to let the staff know, to give them or her stepfather any prior warning, in case there was anything to hide.

How she hated these ludicrous, suspicious thoughts.

She'd forgotten about getting in touch with Ashley, Damon's assistant, but that could wait until she'd searched the house.

The home was located southeast of Bellingham, toward the national forests. Damon had preferred his home near a seaport or an airport, but agreed to move inland to the mansion sitting on the side of a mountain for Regina. Sylvie directed Will, who was clearly enjoying driving the Camaro. If she tried, she could almost imagine they were out for an afternoon joyride to take in the scenery of thick forests. They had been on the road for almost an hour when they hit Marblemount.

"Better stop and get gas here. Not many stops after this. We can grab some snacks, too."

Will filled the tank while Sylvie grabbed sodas and

junk food. She exited the gas station and let herself admire Will as he topped off the gas. She had to admit he looked good standing next to that car. But then she caught the expression on his face.

Something was wrong.

The realization made her trip up as she approached. "What's the matter?"

"Someone's following us," he stated grimly.

"What?" She started to turn—

"Don't look." He leaned in as if he would kiss her, obviously trying to make it look as though they hadn't noticed their tail.

Her breath hitched at his nearness, at how much she wanted him to kiss her. She stepped back and handed off his snacks, gathering her composure. That had been a close call. He was a huge distraction in her efforts to figure this out. Sylvie tried to look nonchalantly across the street as she made her way around the car and climbed in. Once inside she flipped the visor down to look through the mirror but couldn't see anything.

Will pulled out of the gas station and continued onto the state highway.

"Don't turn around, Sylvie. Don't give us away. Let them think we don't know they're back there."

"How long have you known?"

"I've had my suspicions from the start, but the gas station stop more than persuaded me."

She sank down in the seat. "I don't want to lead them to the house and cause problems for my stepfather or anyone there."

"On the contrary, maybe they're letting your stepfather know that you're on the way and to be prepared for you. Don't let your guard down around that man or anyone who works for him. I know you want to believe he's innocent, but at the same time you've more than convinced me he's not."

"He's not even there. But I hear what you're saying. Let's lose the tail anyway."

"Tell me about the road ahead. What am I going to see?"

"A lot of twists and turns as we climb into the mountains. Motorcycle enthusiasts love this road."

Will blew out a breath and grinned. "I think I'm going to love it, too."

"Don't get us killed, Will."

"I'm not going to get us killed. I'm trying to keep you alive. Don't you trust me by now?"

Her throat tightened. That was a loaded question. "You haven't let me down yet."

"They're closing the gap. Before we lose them, can you see their faces? See who it is? Is it Diverman and Rifleman?"

She flipped the visor again. "I can't tell."

"All right, then. Hang on."

Sylvie pressed back into the seat as Will floored the accelerator. "If I punch it enough, I should be able to lose them around this next curve. Turn off on a side road or drive."

They whipped around the mountain curve, and Sylvie got a better look of the rocky ravine below than she wanted. She squeezed her eyes shut, willing the centrifugal force to release her. Will turned off onto a private drive and followed it up.

"I saw them drive by. We'll wait here and see if they backtrack." He found a place to turn the car around and waited.

"Do you think we lost them?"

"I have a feeling they already know where we're going so it probably doesn't matter."

Sylvie didn't like his answer, but she didn't know what else to say. She sat back and waited with Will. Finally, he shifted into gear and eased out of their hiding spot back onto the road. They didn't see the vehicle that had tailed them.

She let him enjoy the twists and turns, squeezed her eyes shut when the road hedged the river gorge. A few miles more and they came to the gated drive to Damon's house, and Sylvie punched in the code to open the gates. "We're going to wait on the other side and make sure nobody comes inside the grounds after us, okay?"

"Works for me." Will drove through and waited for the gate to close behind him.

The men that had followed them earlier drove by slowly on the road. The two men peered out at them but acted casually, as if they were out for a Sunday drive.

"At least it's not Diverman and Rifleman."

Will frowned. "No, it's two more people we need to watch out for. Told you they already knew where we were headed. They look like Feds to me."

"How do you know?"

"I've delivered a few Feds to parts unknown now and then."

Sylvie blew out a breath. She couldn't worry about more men following her now—especially if they might just be law enforcement. She had a bigger problem to face head-on and up ahead. Going through Mom's things in search of incriminating evidence against Damon or proof of his innocence was not going to be easy.

A sour taste rose in her mouth.

Sylvie wasn't sure what she hoped to unearth but anything at all that would give her a clue, a look into what happened, was worth this trip. She remained quiet while Will maneuvered the curves of the two-mile paved and winding driveway to the mansion. She thought about Will's warning that she was taking them into the lion's den, right into the mouth of the lion.

The mansion loomed ahead, resting on the side of a mountain and overlooking the river. To the right was a great steel-enforced deck and helipad. The house was all brick and stone stacked in horizontal and vertical planes and overhangs. Sylvie waited for Will's reaction.

"It looks like something from an Alfred Hitchcock movie." Will chuckled. "I'm sorry if that didn't come out right. I think it's magnificent."

"I think the architect was a Frank Lloyd Wright student. As for Alfred Hitchcock, you're thinking of that movie *North by Northwest*. This is similar to that, yes. Though it's modern-looking, futuristic in some ways, it's a decades-old historical mansion that's been refurbished."

"I had pictured something else altogether." Will shifted in his seat. "You never actually said who your stepfather is. I have the feeling he's someone important."

"Damon Masters is the CEO of Masters Marine Corporation. The great-grandson of the founder."

"Um...wow. Just. Wow. Regina did well for herself when she married."

Sylvie frowned at the comment, but didn't say anything. She knew Will hadn't meant any harm.

"So what exactly does the corporation do? Obviously it has to do with the ocean and seafaring vessels, and I sound like a real idiot."

"It's a marine solutions company. Transportation.

Logistics. International and domestic. A holding company for other marine businesses, as well. And don't ask me more than that because then I'll sound like an idiot. Not saying you did, but then you'll find out how little I really know."

Sylvie's mother had started out as her stepfather's assistant, then eventually married him. Sylvie had wanted no part of the business in that capacity. Sitting in an office all day turned her into a puddle.

Had Will sunk down into his seat?

"And you're the princess." He'd said it matter-of-factly, as though there was no question in his mind.

She bristled at his words but was unsure how to respond. After all, there was truth in them and she'd said as much herself. And that left her torn. Yes, her childhood had been privileged. But that wasn't always a good thing. Money could cover up a lot of ugliness, but it didn't make the pain go away. How could this beautiful old mansion, refurbished and loved, shelter a family that had loved and hated and perhaps even killed? Just what secrets did it harbor?

He slowed the Camaro and parked in the circular drive. The helicopter was parked on the helipad, which overhung a steep cleft in the mountain and had drawn his attention. He shut off the ignition.

"Look at me."

He slowly turned, an entirely unfamiliar expression on his face.

"Don't be intimidated."

He stiffened. "Who said I was?"

"That's why I never tell anyone who my stepfather is."

"Why aren't you involved in his business?"

She'd already told him she was a diving instructor,

but not the details of how and why she ended up getting that job. "The Masters Diving School is one of the subsidiaries. I guess the name gave that away." She shrugged and studied the immaculate grounds. "I guess my biological father's blood runs through me. I'm more interested in getting my hands dirty. Doing hands-on work, like he did with the avalanche center, and as a search and rescue volunteer. I love diving, and teaching others. Volunteering on the search and rescue dives. The rest of it, the business side of a large international corporation, just isn't for me."

Will scraped a hand over his face and around his neck.

"It's okay," she said. "You're going to be fine. Other than the staff, no one is even here. So what are you worried about?"

"This brings everything to a whole new level, Sylvie. Why didn't you tell me?"

"I mentioned he's a powerful man. That he could afford to pay someone to sabotage the plane and send people after me. You didn't believe me?" She watched him. "Don't tell me you're backing out already."

"No. Never. I'm in this until it's over. If I had known it could have helped me to prepare myself. We're in over our heads. What if this is more than murder or a crime of passion that someone wants to keep hidden? Maybe it's corporate espionage stuff. If so, this case is something more for the FBI than local law enforcement, don't you think?"

"Not yet. No, I don't think. I was in Alaska when someone tried to kill me. That doesn't link anything back to my stepfather's corporation." *Per se.* Could her mother have found something out that was bigger than Sylvie had imagined? Something that could have huge repercussions for her stepfather's company? Two men who Will thought were Feds had followed them.

"And yet you're here, at the house, believing you'll find answers to where it all started."

Sylvie couldn't argue with that. She rubbed her eyes then blinked over at Will. "I brought my bodyguard with me."

She'd hoped to elicit a smile, but Will had anything but a smile on his face.

"Men have tried to kill you. This isn't a game."

"I know that. Just... I know that. Consider this a covert operation. Nobody has to even know what I'm looking for. We pretend we're here for a quick getaway..." How else would she explain Will's presence?

She saw the same question in his eyes.

"We'll get in and get out quickly." She hadn't wanted Marguerite, who oversaw the housekeeping and meals, to make a big fuss over her. Though her stepfather's meager security detail would know of her arrival as soon as she'd entered through the gate, she'd try to keep this as low-key as possible.

She opened the door to exit the car, but leaned closer to Will. "We can't sit here all day."

Sylvie climbed out of the car, quietly shut the door then waited for Will. Together they marched up the steps. She feared he might turn around and hightail it back to the car, but she resisted the urge to grab his hand and drag him forward with her. He'd wanted to act as her bodyguard, after all.

Before she reached the massive front door, it swung open and a familiar form stepped into view.

Damon Masters, Sylvie's stepfather.

THIRTEEN

Will grabbed the hand Damon Masters offered after Sylvie performed the introductions. The grip strong and sure, the man measuring Will, just as Will measured him. In his midfifties, Masters exuded the power that one would expect from someone who ran an international corporation. He was also a handsome sort, looking like the type of man that could have any woman he wanted—if not with money and power, then with looks. His dark eyes continued to study Will as he greeted them in a friendly manner. But suspicion and questions lurked behind his gaze aimed at Will.

On the other hand, the man was clearly pleased to see Sylvie. "I didn't realize you'd be here." Her tenuous smile could give them away.

Masters chuckled. "You sound like you're not happy that I'm here."

"Just surprised, that's all. I thought you were supposed to be in Asia."

His eyebrows edged together. "I had to come back for some unexpected business. But there's always a silver lining, isn't there? And you're it. I'm grateful for the serendipitous meeting. Two ships passing in the night.

Unfortunately, I'm tied up with a conference call this evening and then leaving quickly after that, but I'd love to spend a few minutes with you." Behind Masters, a woman entered and smiled at Sylvie, stepping over to give her a hug.

Sylvie's face brightened. "Ashley, it's good to see you."

The young woman, in her early thirties, if that, was stunning. "And you, as well. I just arrived an hour ago, myself. Damon and I needed to prepare for a meeting."

"Would you please have Marguerite bring refreshments?" Masters said.

Ashley's face clouded but she recovered with a quick smile, then disappeared around a corner. Following her with his eyes, Will caught sight of the walls of windows displaying a breathtaking mountainous view.

Will had never seen anything like it, except, well, from his bird's-eye view in the sky when he flew. Sylvie dragged Will through the house after her stepfather, leaning in to whisper, "Ashley's Damon's assistant. She was close to my mother. I can talk to her while she's here."

"There's no need for refreshments," she said next, turning her attention to Masters. "Don't treat me like a guest." Sylvie moved away from Will and stepped down into a sunken, spacious living area with sleek sofas and chairs. She trailed her finger over the spines of books lining the wall.

"I see you so rarely."

"I still have a room here."

Now what? Would Masters block her efforts to go through her mother's things? Or would Sylvie's life be in more danger now? Will wanted to be prepared for anything, but he was pretty sure he wasn't. After everything she'd told him about her stepfather, he'd not been prepared for the man he saw now, nor Sylvie's reaction to him.

"Of course you're not a guest, but your friend is. And either way, I'd like a few minutes with you before I have to leave."

The man headed to the wet bar and poured himself a glass of amber liquid. He glanced over his shoulder. "Something for you, Mr. Pierson?"

"No, thanks."

A woman who Will guessed to be Marguerite entered, holding a tray with two pitchers and fancy snacks that would pass for hors d'oeuvres. "It's a while until dinner, Sylvie. I hadn't expected guests, but I'll be sure to cook something nice for you and your friend."

"Thanks, Marguerite. This will do for now." Sylvie took the glass of lemonade the woman had poured.

She glanced at Will over the rim of her glass as she drank, determination, and not just a little fear, in her eyes. What was she planning? Will preferred the iced tea and drank up, not realizing how thirsty he'd been.

When Marguerite left the room, Masters turned to face them, swirling the liquid in his glass. "Why are you here, Sylvie?"

She set the glass on the tray. "I want to finally go through Mom's things."

"I'm afraid you're too late. I've had Ashley box them up and put them in storage."

Will imagined he felt Sylvie's pain. The man had sounded so cold with his pronouncement. Why hadn't he gone through her things himself? Treasuring each item, remembering his wife with each touch? And for that matter, what was the rush? The plane crash had been only two months before. Something definitely seemed off here. Except Will had yet to do that with his mother's things. He'd left everything in her home just as it was. He'd needed closure first. Needed to find the plane. Find his mother.

"How could you? You knew I wanted to go through them."

"It's been two months."

"Where are the boxes, then?"

"What's really going on, Sylvie? You can't expect me to believe you brought a stranger here to go through your mother's belongings with you." He eyed the two of them.

Will bristled.

"I think someone murdered her. I want to look through her stuff to see if I can find any clues to find who might have wanted to hurt her."

Will set his glass on the tray and moved to stand by Sylvie. Apparently, she wasn't all that great at the covert operations she'd mentioned. No matter, he'd stand by her regardless.

Masters set his glass down, too, his gaze slowly darkening. Then, in an instant, concern replaced anger. He moved to Sylvie and took one of her hands in both of his. "You're still grieving, Sylvie. Of course you are. It's only been a couple of months. I'm struggling to accept her death, as well. Please, sit down."

Sylvie surprised Will by doing as her stepfather instructed. Did the man still have so much sway over her?

When Masters sat next to Sylvie on the sofa, Will felt like the proverbial awkward third wheel and might have left the room, leaving them to have their private conversation. Except Will believed Sylvie was in danger, even from her stepfather. Especially from her stepfather. It was easy enough for him to be wary of the man, but he understood how torn Sylvie must be.

"I can arrange for you to see a therapist," Masters said. "The best in the country. I'm so sorry I didn't realize how hard this has been on you. But I know you. You keep it all inside. You wouldn't have shared it with me before this moment, even if there'd been an opportunity."

"I've been afraid that you were involved."

Masters flinched as though he'd been slapped.

Will wondered if he should intervene, but had no clue how to do it. Better to let things play out. He wished he had a weapon with him, if Sylvie's stepfather was the threat she believed.

The man glanced at Will. "Could you give us some privacy, Mr. Pierson?"

Um...no. "I need to stay."

Masters gave a slight nod, letting Will know he wouldn't be underestimated. Then Masters turned his attention back to Sylvie, as if she were a stepdaughter he clearly loved as his own. "That's ridiculous. Shocking. I'm not sure how to respond, except I wish I could cancel my meeting and stay here with you. Of course... *of course* I didn't kill Regina. How could you think it for one second? She was my wife and yes, we argued, had our problems, but I loved her. I could never murder anyone, especially my wife. Someone I loved. She died in a plane crash, Sylvie. It's tragic, but it happens to people every day. There was no murder. What has gotten into you?"

The man sounded sincere. But didn't crimes of passion—murder of a spouse—make up for a big percentage of the world's murders every year? Even if he truly had loved his wife, that didn't mean he hadn't killed her.

"I have enough problems with everything going on at…" Masters didn't finish. Instead, he inched away from Sylvie and leaned against the sofa back. With a haggard expression Will imagined not many had seen the powerful man show, he swiped his hands down his face and stared at the carpet.

Tears slid down Sylvie's cheeks. Will wanted to be the one sitting there next to her so he could comfort her. Was she being manipulated and influenced by Masters? Was he putting on an act?

"Your mother wasn't murdered, Sylvie. I'm going to call someone who can help you realize that." Masters stood and reached for his cell.

What was happening here? Their plans were crumbling before Will's eyes. Did he even have a clue what he'd walked into with Sylvie? He took a step forward, dark thoughts pushing him into dangerous territory. Did her stepfather have the power to whisk Sylvie away and have her institutionalized? He'd heard stories about how people were locked up by their families and never got out.

Sylvie grabbed the cell away from him. "You're not listening. Someone's trying to kill me."

Masters glanced at Will for confirmation. He was in it now. No going back. He nodded. "It's true. She didn't dream this up. I intervened when I saw someone attacking her. One of my friends was killed in the crossfire." Will left out that Sylvie had been shot, too. He'd let Sylvie tell the man if she wanted him to know.

"Then you need protection." Frowning at Will, Masters took his cell back. "Real protection."

Cell to his ear, he spoke to Sylvie. "And the police should be involved."

"They already are," she said. "The Alaskan State Troopers are handling the case."

"You'll need a bodyguard. I'll hire an investigator if the police can't get to the bottom of this." He turned his back on them to speak into his cell.

Sylvie stood and rushed to Will. Things were taking a completely different turn than they'd expected. By the expression on Sylvie's face, she didn't like it, either.

"What's happening?" Will whispered. The question was stupid, but he didn't know how to react. Was this a good thing or a bad thing? Did she believe her stepfather was innocent now?

Sylvie leaned in as though she would give Will a peck on the cheek and whispered, "Just go with it, Will."

Masters ended his call and turned his attention to them. "I've got people on it. Stay at the house, Sylvie. There's no reason for you to leave until your life is no longer at risk. You're more than welcome to stay as well, Mr. Pierson, though I imagine you have a job you need to return to."

Will grinned. He was self-employed, which meant he had to work harder, but it also meant that he decided when he worked. And right now he wouldn't let Masters get rid of him so easily. "I'm with Sylvie until I know she's safe."

The man ignored Will and gave Sylvie a hug, then grabbed her shoulders and looked her in the eyes. "I don't want you hurt, do you hear me? I need you to promise you won't leave the house until I've resolved this."

"I have a job, too."

"In a roundabout way, you work for me, remember?"

"I don't want you to intervene. I don't want your favors there. Officially, I'm on vacation right now. This will be over before I have to go back."

"You'll stay?"

"Yes, I'll stay."

"Good. I'll take care of things. I know you don't like to hear that. You've always been so independent, but we're talking about your life." He stepped back, tucked his chin. "Please tell me that you don't think I murdered your mother. That you don't think I would try to kill you."

The man appeared genuinely crestfallen.

"I know you didn't. You're right. I've been upset about her death. I've not been thinking clearly these past couple of months. And now I'm scared for my life." Sylvie pressed her hand over her mouth a moment then dropped it. "Thank you for your help."

"I hope you'll never hesitate to come to me in the future. And... Sylvie—" he stood taller, like a man who'd taken control back "—don't bother looking for your mother's things. That would only upset you more. Fortunately, they've been packed away and I doubt you could easily find them. Don't bother enlisting Marguerite's help. I'm leaving her with strict instructions about that. I suggest waiting until you feel better. I'll make them available to you then. Please, try to get some rest while you're here." His gaze found Will. "I'm trusting you to keep her occupied if you stay. There's plenty to do here. A heated pool. Trails to hike. Just stay close to the house and take the bodyguard even if you're staying on the grounds. I've already made the arrangements. Protection is on the way."

He headed for the door then turned back to them. "If I didn't have this mess on my hands, I'd stay here with you."

"What mess?" Sylvie asked.

"I'll explain everything when it's over. There's too much at stake and I have to go. I'll be back as soon as I can."

And with that, the man was gone, leaving Will alone with Sylvie, his head spinning with the power the man wielded. Too much at stake. Something bigger than Sylvie's life? "Why did you agree to stay?"

She shook her head. "I don't know. What was I supposed to do?"

"You manipulated him."

"Same as he worked me. If he thinks I'm tucked away safely here and that I believe he's innocent, then we'll have more opportunity to search for my mother's things."

"What do you believe, Sylvie? Is he involved or not? He could be trying to hold us prisoner here while he cleans up this mess. For all we know, we're part of the mess he wants to clean up, and that's why he's pushing for us to stay where he can get to us."

"You could be right. Or we could wait here where we'll be protected by the bodyguard he called and a private investigator searches for the truth for us."

"You're talking weeks. Months. And that's only if we actually trust the investigator and bodyguard to do their jobs."

"I'm talking tonight. We're not waiting around for anybody. We're going through my mother's things tonight, after my stepfather is gone, and then we'll get out."

* * *

In her old room she sank onto the bed. Seeing Damon had shaken her, but his preoccupation with business troubles would give her the chance she needed to search. She and Will enjoyed a quick and simple pasta meal Marguerite had prepared, eating alone while her stepfather and Ashley took their conference call and then prepared to leave. This was a lot of work for after-hours. But with an international corporation, it was always business hours somewhere in the world.

Although there wasn't anyone to watch her, she made a show of unpacking and then putting away the few items she'd brought, as though she had every intention of staying in her old room like she'd told her stepfather. Like she was a little girl again—a princess—as Will had put it.

Sylvie wasn't a princess. She was a woman on a mission who'd dragged an unintentional hero along with her. In keeping with their ruse, Will was in one of the guest rooms at the far end of the hallway. Not too far. And yet, entirely too close.

Part of her wished she hadn't needed his presence to chase away her fears. Regardless, they were both in it deep now, if they hadn't been before. There wasn't a moment to lose or any time to let her guard down, especially now that she'd revealed so much to Damon.

With his reaction, he'd made her doubt every conclusion she'd reached. When she'd seen him in the doorway, she hadn't known what to do or expect. Had no idea why she'd blurted out the truth, but she'd desperately wanted to know if he was involved, had been willing to risk hers and Will's lives to know the truth about the man who had raised her.

A chill ran over her.

She hadn't liked what she'd seen behind his gaze. He was hiding something. Something was terribly wrong but Sylvie couldn't tell if it was related to company woes, as he'd mentioned, or her accusations. But Ashley, his assistant and her mother's friend, was here, too. Despite the fact Sylvie hadn't wanted to see Damon, she'd been glad to see Ashley. If only she would get the chance to speak to her privately before she left.

The thrum of a helicopter drew Sylvie to the window. Darkness had taken hold, but lights kept the helipad well lit. Ashley at his side, Damon hurried toward the helicopter that would deliver them to their meeting. But then they paused, appearing deep in conversation.

There was a soft knock on the door. Probably Marguerite, coming to ask if she needed anything more before retiring to her own room. Sylvie had grown accustomed to living on her own. No maids or staff hovering, watching her every move. It had been surprisingly easy to get used to. Sylvie craved freedom and privacy. She swung the door open. Will stood on the other side.

"Sylvie—"

She yanked him into the room and closed the door. "Keep your voice down."

"Why all the cloak and dagger?"

"Because I'm supposed to be in bed already. I'm tired, remember? You, too."

"You told me you'd come get me in a few minutes. It's been half an hour. I got worried."

"Honestly, I needed a few minutes to myself. Being here is hard. Seeing him drained me."

"Since we're being honest, I've been in the hallway outside your door, standing guard. I got tired of waiting."

Watching him lean against the door now, anxiety in his eyes mixed with concern for her, warmth tingled through her belly. A feeling she couldn't ignore. A feeling she couldn't afford.

She turned her back rather than risking that he'd see her face and read the thoughts rushing through her silly-girl head. Rubbing her temples as if thinking things through, she said, "We have to get to work before the bodyguard shows up in case Damon has instructed him to spy on us or stop us. I've been waiting for the helicopter to leave with him. I don't want Marguerite to know what we're up to, either."

"What's your plan, then?" Will's voice was close behind her.

Without looking at him, she moved to the window again, watching for any sign of a vehicle arriving with a bodyguard.

"We head for the basement."

"The basement?"

"That's my first stop to find the boxes with Mom's stuff." Sylvie turned, ready to escape the room and the memories that rushed at her. "That's one of the big differences in a regular house and a Frank Lloyd Wright house. His houses had no basements or attics."

Will stood in her way, grabbed her shoulders. "I don't care about Frank what's-his-name. I care about you and this situation. I have a bad feeling about this. We're risking too much by just being here. Your stepfather was right about one thing. This can't be easy on you. It must be hard to think he could murder your mother."

"Hard enough hearing the arguments they had over the years. Knowing that he cheated on her."

Sylvie couldn't look at him anymore and rushed to

the door. What he must be thinking—that her mother deserved to be cheated on, considering Sylvie was the product of an adulterous relationship. All of it serving as a reminder to Sylvie that she couldn't go through that kind of pain, loving a man and getting married. Couldn't expose herself to that kind of hurt. The reminder was good timing, helping her keep her heart distanced from the man standing just behind her, his concern for her resounding in his panicked breaths.

Placing her hand against the knob, she spoke softly, "Let's get this over with."

The sooner she discovered the truth and exposed it, the sooner she could put safe distance between her and Will Pierson.

FOURTEEN

What would a basement inside a place like this look like? Will wasn't sure he wanted to find out. Didn't want to go down in the dark and be trapped if someone tried to attack them again.

As far as Will was concerned, the longer they stayed, the greater the danger, now that Damon Masters himself knew they were here.

Trailing Sylvie down the hallway, Will fought the urge to creep around like a couple of criminals. Just like Sylvie, he wanted to find out what really happened to his mother. But since their arrival here, he was beginning to think that Sylvie was leading them on a wild goose chase. Surely Masters would have destroyed any evidence against him rather than packing it away in the basement. Still, he couldn't bring himself to tell Sylvie that. Instead, he followed her around like a puppy. Hadn't he been here before? Following Michelle around? Whoa…what was he doing, comparing the two women? He'd been in love with Michelle. He and Sylvie were trying to solve a murder together and stay alive while they were at it.

He should ask the obvious question. Should have

asked a long time ago. "Why would your stepfather leave anything incriminating in your mother's things if he thought she had something to hide and had killed her for it? I'm thinking that's the main reason he had the stuff boxed up and put away before you got to it—so he could go through it and get rid of anything problematic."

She cast him a glare. "I don't want to believe my stepfather is a murderer, and that's why I'm here to find out who is responsible. But you're right, if he is involved he would... Wait... He had Ashley do it."

"So he says."

"Look, it's the best place to start."

"But you were looking for the plane first—you thought that was the right place to start."

"I went looking for the plane so I could find out what happened. If I found it then I could let the authorities know and they could see if it looked like foul play. I was only working on the slightest suspicion. Now that I have a strong reason to believe that it wasn't an accident, I need to see her things. Make sense?" Sylvie paused and turned to face him. "Why are you asking me this now? If you didn't want to come along, you could have said so earlier. I told you I didn't need your help."

Disappointment flickered in her eyes. Will wanted to kick himself. "I'm here, aren't I? I told you I'd see this through with you. I'm just thinking out loud, is all. The basement doesn't seem like a good idea to me. What could you hope to find?"

Turning her back on him, she started down again. "I can't tell you what I'm looking for. Only that I'll know it when I see it."

At the end of the hallway, Will followed her down a spiraling wrought-iron staircase that seemed as at odds with the stark lines of the home's architecture as he was with Sylvie at the moment.

With each step drawing them closer to the basement, Will's concern for her increased. "Your stepfather told you not to look for your mother's things. It might be too upsetting. Are you sure about this, Sylvie?"

At the bottom, she turned on him. "He wouldn't be the man he is today if he wasn't skilled in the power of persuasion. He's very convincing. I've listened to him persuade my mother that he loved her and only her and would never cheat on her." Her voice cracked.

Her pain was palpable, and he wanted to take her hand and squeeze it. Reassure her. Instead, he whispered, "Sylvie..." And with that one breath he conveyed all the turmoil and emotions he felt about their situation. About Sylvie. But he didn't know how to comfort her, or if that was even something she wanted from him.

She had a smudge on her cheek and for some reason Will couldn't fathom, he reached up and pressed his thumb against the silk of her skin and wiped it away. An innocent-enough motion, but it somehow had his breaths coming faster. And sent his heart into his throat.

Sylvie inched back, wiping the moment away. "Okay, the basement is just down another flight of stairs."

Will followed her, descending a slim and dank staircase. Everything beyond the spiral staircase looked as if it belonged to a different house entirely. A different century, even. Sylvie slowed as she approached. A single bulb flickered from the ceiling. She took the last three steps to stand in front of the door and tried the knob.

"It's locked. I should have known."

"There's a chair here, too. Would he have a guard on the door to keep you out?"

"I don't know what to think."

"Well, if there was a guard here, he might be back soon. We need to hurry."

Pulling out his pocketknife, Will tried to work the lock free, but the dead bolt was obviously engaged. "Why not ask for a key?"

"You heard him. He didn't want me in her things. I can't ask for a key. All the more reason for me to look."

Sylvie's stepfather had told her to stay away, so she would do the opposite. "I'm not sure what's worse. That what you just said makes some kind of sense to me or that the door is locked and our whole reason for coming is shot."

Sylvie scraped her hands through her hair. "Being in this house drains me. I can't think straight. That's why I moved out and went to work doing what I love. But down here in the dark and dank, I feel like the walls are closing in on me."

Will could relate. "What now?"

She cocked her head. "Do you hear footsteps?" she whispered. "Someone is coming down the stairs."

"If it's the same someone who is guarding the door we can ask for a key." He grinned, but only to bring levity to the moment. He didn't like this one bit.

Someone was definitely creeping down the steps, their footfalls soft.

Panic swirled in Sylvie's eyes. "There's no place to hide."

"We're not going to hide anymore. We're going to walk up the stairs like we have every right to be here." Will would go first in case this house harbored the villains after Sylvie.

On the next corner, he came face-to-face with Marguerite, who stood two steps above him. She gasped, covered her mouth and let out a stream of words in French.

Sylvie pushed by Will and hugged Marguerite to her. "You scared us to death. Marguerite, we need to get in the basement."

"I thought I might find you down here when you didn't answer your door. You cannot be here, Sylvie. I don't have the key, and even if I did, I would be afraid to help you."

Sylvie released Marguerite, a woman she'd known almost her entire life. "Why do you say that, Marguerite? Please tell me. I need to know everything. Do you know what happened to my mother?"

The woman shook her head vehemently. She pressed a finger to her lips. "The house has ears, too many ears," she whispered.

"I'm not leaving until I get into the basement."

Marguerite's eyes grew wide. "Of course! Do you not remember you grew up in this house? Back then, you had your own secret passages."

Sylvie's face scrunched up.

"Of course I knew about them. You think I wouldn't know?"

"Thank you for reminding me." Sylvie kissed Marguerite on the cheek then looked at Will. "I used to get into the basement all the time. I had my own secret way in. Why didn't I think of that before?"

Sounded like the house really was closing in on her and choking her thoughts.

"Probably because you weren't thinking you'd need a secret passage as an adult." He was glad they hadn't faced some new threat on the stairwell. "Lead on."

"Wait." Marguerite stood in Sylvie's path. "Be careful. There have been strangers here. More than that, I cannot tell you. Make your search quick and then please leave. Promise me."

"Of course," Sylvie whispered. "I promise. And thank you, Marguerite, for your help. Now promise me you'll go back to your room. I don't want you involved."

"Don't worry about me. Unless they need something from me, I'm only the help and invisible to the strangers. Even to your stepfather."

Sylvie and Will waited until Marguerite had disappeared before they continued on. Once it was quiet again, Sylvie led him to the top of the stairwell where they ducked into a dark closet that smelled of pine-based cleaning supplies. She turned on the light and bent over. Started removing the boxes beneath a shelf.

"See? An old laundry chute. The laundry wasn't done down there anymore, even when I was a child, and this was closed off and forgotten. I'm so glad I ran into Marguerite."

If she expected Will to climb down that, she might need to think again. It would be a close fit, if he could do it at all. The thought of crawling through that tight space made him shudder. "Isn't that kind of far for a child to slide?"

Sylvie rummaged around, looking for something in old boxes. He had a hard time seeing her as the kind of child to play in a basement, given her love of the water and diving—a wide-open space she could explore. Just like the skies were for him. His only use for big bodies of water came in landing his plane.

"Found it. I can hardly believe it's still here, but I guess looking at all the rest of this junk, it makes sense." She held up a fire escape ladder. "My mom made sure I had a ladder I could hang from my window in case of a fire."

"That's good emergency protocol."

"I found another use for the ladder."

Sylvie unfolded the ladder to its full length, let it drop down into the laundry chute, and hooked it in place. Will felt silly. But if there was no other way into the basement without that key, then...

"I'll go down first," he said.

"I don't need a hero, Will."

"Sure you do." He grinned then made sure the thing was secure.

At Sylvie's wide-eyed stare, he almost laughed. He had an innate urge to plant a kiss on her lips that had formed into a half frown, half smile. He could tell she didn't know what to make of him. "We're in this together, remember?"

Before she could argue he disappeared down the ladder, hoping a big load of trouble wasn't waiting for him at the bottom. Will climbed down as far as he could but then the ladder ended. How much farther was the drop? Sylvie said she'd done this as a child. He should be okay to let go and fall then, but it was dark down there. He had no idea what he was dropping onto or into.

He squeezed his eyes shut. *Lord, help me out here?*

"Will?" Sylvie whispered.

"Yes?"

"Are you okay? What are you doing? I need to come down, too."

"I'm working up the courage to drop into the unknown."

"The ladder doesn't go all the way?"

"No. Maybe you don't remember exactly how this worked."

"I remember that ladder went all the way. But if you want me to go first, I'll go. I told you I didn't need a hero."

"Especially if he's dead," he mumbled.

"What's that?"

"Nothing." Will let go and slowed his progress with his feet and hands as he slid the rest of the way. As he neared the bottom, he could finally see his surroundings. Someone had left a dim light on. Will didn't care why, only that it lit his way enough.

Beneath him boxes were stacked high. He could drop and hopefully stand on them, or fall and get hurt. He slowly lowered himself onto the first box. Held on to the rim of the laundry chute then grabbed on to a beam while he got his bearings, put more weight on the box. He bounced a little to get the feel of it.

Then he heard Sylvie making her way down. Oh, no. He wasn't prepared for that yet.

"Wait up," he said into the laundry chute.

Will climbed down, removed the boxes from beneath the chute and found the sturdiest-looking old chair. He stood on that to catch Sylvie. "Okay, careful coming down."

Sylvie slid down the chute rather than crawling out, which surprised him. She would land hard. Then she appeared, popping out, and Will caught her in his arms, surprising them both.

"Will!" she gasped his name.

And he laughed.

The chair collapsed beneath them.

Will kept his balance and her in his arms. "Are you okay?" she asked.

The chair lay splintered on the floor. He was entirely

too close, the masculine scent of him wrapping around her and making her dizzy. Making her feel things she didn't want to feel.

"Yeah, but I think we might have woken the dead."

"We don't need to worry about them. It's the living we should worry about. The guard, if there is one, outside the door."

"Which brings me to a question I should have asked before we made this leap of faith down the laundry chute," Will replied.

Sylvie studied the mess in the basement. What looked like old IKEA furniture was piled high, along with the wooden chair Will had just broken. Her spirits sank. She couldn't imagine someone actually storing her mother's things in the basement. "So what's your question?"

"You climbed down here as a child. How did you get out? Because there's no way we are climbing back up."

"Oops. I hadn't thought of that." At Will's grimace she laughed. "We go out the door. It's locked from the outside to keep people from getting in. But it can be unlocked from the inside to prevent someone from accidentally being locked down here."

Sheer relief registered on Will's face, along with a day's worth of stubble. His beard would grow thick and fast, by the looks of it, if he didn't shave every day. Why was she thinking about that? She pulled her gaze from Will's features in the dim lighting and glanced around the basement. Where to start?

"I remember it being much brighter down here when I used to play." Now it was dark and gloomy. Cobwebs hung in every possible place. Where were the spiders that had left all these? Still alive and well? Her skin crawled. "There's another light somewhere. You can be a hero now, Will, and find it. Knock down some of those webs, too."

Something unseen skittered away in the corner. Sylvie froze. Locked gazes with Will. Humor shimmered in his warm eyes, but understanding gleamed there also. "I don't like cold, dark spaces with spiderwebs, either, especially when other vermin can be heard vying for front-row seats."

"Very funny." She had no plans to entertain the rats.

"Why do you think I love to fly? You never see a web in the sky. Or spiders, for that matter."

"No cobwebs in the water when I go diving." But the thought reminded her of her mother's plane and what it might look like with the passing years if no one discovered it. They had to get busy.

Sylvie had never been afraid of the dark, but she couldn't shake the images of creepy creatures with any number of legs lurking in the shadowed corners. To his credit, Will grabbed a broom and scraped a few silken, dusty webs down. Since there was a small lamp on in the corner, Sylvie wondered who had been down here and why hadn't they disturbed the webs. The lamp might mean that someone had, in fact, brought her mother's things down.

Together they searched the basement, which seemed to go on forever. Someone needed to take this old rubbish to the Dumpster, and the decent furniture to the Salvation Army. Finally, she found some newer-looking plastic bins stacked among old cardboard boxes stained with rat droppings.

Her skin crawled again, and she sneezed. If Ashley had actually put all her mother's things down here...

Sylvie would be furious. Sylvie switched on an overhead light and started looking at the bins, hoping they
were labeled. Will searched on the fringe with a flashlight he'd found.

The way dirt and dust had been disturbed, someone
else had been here recently doing something more than
turning on a lamp.

"I found something," Will said.

Sylvie left the bin she was examining and made her
way to him, bumping into the corner of an old desk.
"What'd you find?"

He held up an old pocketknife.

The breath whooshed from her. "Can you be serious and help me?"

"You never know when one of these is going to come
in handy. I lost the one I carried."

The knob jiggled; keys jingled.

Sylvie stared at Will. Panic gripped her stomach.
"What do we do?"

"Just tell them what we're doing?"

"We can't do that. You heard Marguerite. There are
strangers in the house. We can't trust them." Sylvie
grabbed Will's hand and dragged him deeper, behind
stacks of boxes. She yanked the chain, switching off the
light in that part of the basement. The only light on now
was the lamp near the door that had been on when they'd
arrived. Backed into a dark corner, something tickled
in her hair and she pushed down the scream threatening to erupt. Shoving away the webs she'd backed into
and the possible spider that went with them, her skin
crawled at the thought of the little creepers.

She'd give anything if she could run out of the basement screaming and shaking her hair free of creeping

things. Sylvie dragged in the breaths before it was too late. In, out. In, out.

I can do this.

Spiders are just tiny animals. They don't want to hurt me.

Will wrapped his arm around her and leaned in close. His warm breath fanned her hair. What? The webs didn't bother him? Apparently not. She let his presence calm her nerves. Together they waited and watched. The door opened and heavy footsteps clomped around while larger-than-life shadows fell across the walls from the dim light of the lamp. The beam from a flashlight danced along the rafters and ceiling.

The laundry chute door hung open.

Sylvie almost gasped.

Would the man notice? Become suspicious?

Will was right. This was just plain stupid to hide like children who'd been caught. They should face this man head-on and get their answers. Sylvie would rather face him than stay in the spiderwebs. She started to move from Will's grasp, but he held her in place. She glanced at him. He pressed a finger against his lips and motioned for her to look through a space between the boxes.

From there, she could see the man—he was the one who'd pretended to be a nurse at the hospital in order to kill her. She would never forget his dark, sinister eyes. It was Diverman.

FIFTEEN

Will stiffened when Sylvie sucked in a breath. That had been much too loud. He held his breath. Stood perfectly still.

Had the man heard?

Seconds ticked by.

Carefully, Will peeked through the boxes again. The man stood stock-still. Listening. He'd heard something, all right. Will wished the rodents would make their presence known. Maybe that would distract the man.

Will wanted to rush from where they were hiding and tackle the man while he had the element of surprise. Secure him and call the police. Get the answers they needed. But he spotted the man's weapon tucked in his pants and he didn't want to put Sylvie at more risk than she already was. She'd been shot once before, and Will couldn't let that happen again.

But if Diverman decided to search, the two of them would be discovered. Jumping the man might be his only choice. He just wasn't sure how to achieve that. Will would have to wait until the man drew closer and they could push the stacks of boxes over on him. Gain the upper hand. Will couldn't risk communicating his plans to Sylvie and hoped she understood. From where he stood, he scanned the boxes, looking for the best angle. Wishing the guy would come closer and yet hoping he would simply leave.

Shining the flashlight in the corners, the man crept forward, frowning at the cobwebs, too. Will swallowed, sent up a silent prayer and prepared to storm the boxes, toppling them over.

Then someone called the man from the doorway. Was it Marguerite? She'd just saved them. The man switched off the lights, closed the door behind him, leaving them in utter darkness. Will and Sylvie expelled a collective breath.

"That was too close," she whispered.

"I was about to tackle him." His pulse still sky high from the close encounter, Will reached for Sylvie and pulled her to him. Reflex. Pure reflex.

Her heart pounded against the crush of his chest, and he held her until she calmed. Until they both did. "Diverman is here, and probably Rifleman, too. Now we know who the strangers are and that this is the worst-case scenario. We have to leave."

There could be no doubt her stepfather was involved in the attacks against them. Will couldn't imagine what that knowledge, that confirmation, did to Sylvie, who'd been hoping to prove otherwise. But what way the man was involved, Will couldn't be sure. He still couldn't fathom the man who'd been so concerned for his stepdaughter would want her dead. Send men to kill her. Was Diverman the bodyguard that he'd called?

"But I haven't gone through the boxes yet. I'm not leaving until I find something I can use to…" Her voice shook as she trailed off.

Neither of them wanted to say the words. Too harsh. Too cruel.

Sylvie felt around and found the chain and yanked the light on.

"I don't think your stepfather would have left anything of value in the boxes."

"But why did Diverman come down here, then? Maybe…maybe now that my stepfather knows I want to look in the boxes, he must have sent this man to remove them."

Will gripped her shoulders. "The man is here at this house to kill you, Sylvie. He could be back down here at any moment, as soon as he learns you are not in your room."

And Will had let her come here, into the lion's den. Like he could have stopped her.

"Don't you see?" he added, hoping she'd understand the urgency. "There's no time to search."

"You're right. Now that Diverman is here, we know something we hadn't known for certain before. But I don't get it. Why hasn't he already tried to kill me? He has to know I'm here."

"Maybe he planned his attack for tonight when you'd be sleeping. Could be he was in your room looking for you already."

Sylvie pressed her hand to her forehead. "Of course. That's it. My death needs to look like an accident, *and* needs to happen far away from the mansion. Killing me here would raise too many questions and a possible investigation that my stepfather doesn't need. But if I had died in a diving accident like I was supposed to, then that would have been the end of it. Even in the hospital, you said he tried to inject me with something first. Using his gun was his last resort."

"Come on, then. Let's get out of here." Will grabbed her hand and headed to the door.

"If I had left well enough alone, just let my mother's death and plane rest at the bottom of that channel, then this wouldn't be happening. You wouldn't be in danger, either." She sighed. "We need to call the police."

"I don't plan on hanging around long enough to make that call until we're at a safe distance."

"Agreed. Let's turn this light off so they won't know we've been down here. Maybe I'll get another chance to look sometime later."

Sylvie yanked the chain, throwing them back into complete darkness.

"I think I remember the layout of the basement," he said.

"Let me lead." Sylvie tugged him to follow. "I could find my way out of here in a blindfold."

Following Sylvie, he only stumbled once as they made their way to the door. When they got there, Will pressed his hand over Sylvie's on the dead bolt. "What if he's on the other side of the door, sitting in the chair we found?"

"He didn't strike me as the sort of guy to sit and guard a basement."

Nevertheless, Will felt along the wall for something hard—a brick. Just in case the small pocketknife wasn't enough.

"Ready?" she whispered.

"Yes."

She gently turned the dead bolt. They both stood in

silence. Waiting and listening to any reaction on the other side. Will stepped in front of Sylvie and opened the door, prepared to use the brick, but no one was there.

"Come on." He led the way as they hurried up the steps with as much stealth as possible until they made it to the wrought-iron spiral staircase. This house was a veritable maze. When they made it to the main floor, Will headed for the front door, but Sylvie held him back.

"Wait," she whispered. "Where are you going?"

"Out."

"I need my purse, my wallet, bank card, and don't forget the keys from your room. We aren't going anywhere without those."

"Hurry, then." Will kept close to Sylvie as they crept up another set of steps, and felt like the eyes from the old Masters family portraits were watching. He held tight to the brick. What he wouldn't give to have a real weapon.

Together they walked by the room Will would have slept in if they were staying. He opened the door and flipped on the lights, prepared to face off with Diverman. He snatched his keys from the dresser and the small pack he'd brought and together they headed to Sylvie's room.

Reaching for the door she paused and looked at Will, caution in her gaze. Would Diverman be inside, waiting for her? If so, Will would be there to stop him this time, just as he had twice before. He urged her out of the way and shoved through the door, prepared to protect her.

Cautiously, they entered the room. When it appeared empty, Sylvie slipped by Will and went for the bed to grab her purse.

A woman stood at the window, with her back to them.

* * *

Ashley turned from the window.

"What are you doing here?" Sylvie glanced at Will. They had believed the room empty. "I thought you left with Damon."

Come to think of it, she hadn't actually seen Ashley leave. Should Sylvie tell Ashley about Diverman? None of them were safe here. But something in the subtle shake of Will's head let her know he was advocating caution. They didn't know whom they could trust.

Not yet.

Ashley rushed to Sylvie's side, her smile tenuous. "I was supposed to go. But we both agreed that I should stay and make sure you're okay until the bodyguard arrives. And when I found your room empty I was more than worried. Where have you been?"

Her gaze leaped from Sylvie to Will as she rubbed her forefinger over the edge of an envelope she held.

"Just showing Will around the house. What's going on, Ashley?" Sylvie eyed the envelope.

Ashley hesitated, studying Will.

"It's okay. You can talk in front of him."

The woman nodded. "The company is in trouble, or else Damon...your stepfather would have stayed here with you himself. But this gave me the opportunity I needed to speak with you."

Sylvie released a sigh. "Oh, good. I had wanted to talk to you, too. But you start—what did you want to tell me?"

"Since we were friends, your stepfather had me box your mother's things away a few weeks ago. I was here working with him, along with the others, on a specific project for a weekend work retreat, if you can imagine that. He was too heartbroken to face it. You can blame me, if you want. I'm the one who persuaded him to let me. I worked on the bedroom first and those things are in boxes in the basement. I hadn't started on her office until last week, and that's when I found this letter addressed to you."

Sylvie's heart jumped. "A letter?" *Why not an email? Or a phone call?* But then her mother *had* called her before she left and given her a vague warning.

Ashley handed the envelope over. "I'm sorry I hadn't gotten it to you sooner. It has a stamp. Obviously, your mother intended to mail it. Maybe she changed her mind. I probably should have mailed it as soon as I found it, but given the circumstances I thought I should deliver it personally. And here you are."

Sylvie held the envelope, wanting to tear into it. "And you haven't opened it?"

"No. Of course not. But Sylvie, I know that she was…"

"What? Tell me."

"Scared." Ashley moved back to the window and stood against the wall, looking out as though she feared someone watched them.

"Scared of what or who? Did you tell the police?" Will asked.

"Yes. I told a detective that she was scared. Left in a hurry and then died in a plane crash."

Sylvie understood the frustration in Ashley's voice and found a measure of reassurance that she and Will weren't alone in their suspicions that there was something sinister about her mother's death. But Sylvie also knew that, in the end, the authorities did not seem to suspect foul play. They were treating the attack on Sylvie as an unrelated incident. Without a plane or bodies, nothing was being done to satisfy Sylvie regarding her and Will's mothers' deaths.

She ripped open the envelope and reached for the letter inside.

"I'm just going to wait out here in the hall," Ashley said.

"There's no need. You can stay."

"No, I think you should have privacy. I'll be right out here. Who knows, maybe that bodyguard will arrive."

She glanced at Will as she moved to the door.

"I'm staying," he said.

Nodding, she slipped outside into the hall. Will rushed to Sylvie, who turned her back to him. She wanted to read the letter alone.

"Sylvie, what are you doing? Let's take the letter with us. We can read it once we're somewhere safe."

"Somewhere safe? Where would that be?" She hated the defensiveness in her voice. "I can't wait one second longer. This could be the key to everything."

"Or the key to nothing. A ploy to keep you here."

She unfolded the letter to see that it had been neatly printed out instead of in her mother's flowing handwriting. "We're safe at the moment with Ashley here, at least until the bodyguard arrives. Diverman won't act with witnesses."

"Really? Remember what happened on the ferry?" Will paced the room.

"Nothing can happen here, at my stepfather's house, that would bring him into question." At least that's what she was counting on at the moment.

Rotor blades resounded outside, the helicopter returning to the mansion after dropping her father at the airport. She tried to push the distractions away so she could focus on her mother's letter to her. Will thrust his hand through his hair and blew out a breath. His pacing would drive her nuts, but Sylvie focused on the letter.

Sylvie,

I've tried so many times to share this with you, but I didn't know how. Despite my troubles with Damon, he's been a good father to you. I haven't wanted to destroy that relationship. But now I fear for my life and I must warn you, as well. I've written this out to mail to you instead of sending an email that could be too easily discovered, recovered on the hard drive. I've found incriminating evidence against my husband, Damon, your stepfather, on an international scale.

I have the information saved on a thumb drive and have kept it with me. It is worth millions of dollars, far more than my life to some. I don't know who I can trust, who to turn to with the information. I cannot trust the police here—Damon has too much influence for me to believe they'd seriously investigate him. I'm being followed and I need to get somewhere safe. I have a friend from Mountain Cove whom I've stayed in touch with all these years. The same friend who helped me to leave over twenty years ago—a bush pilot, Margaret Pierson. I've resented the people of Mountain Cove for too long. Have hated the place and at the same time I've longed to return. From there I'll contact the authorities. I know I'll be safe in Mountain Cove. No one would ever guess I would return there.

And once I'm done with this—once we're through with this—I could rebuild my life on my father's property. But in the meantime, I wanted

to warn you to keep safe. Warn you in case the
worst happened to me so that you would know.
Love,
Mom

Sylvie pressed the letter to her heart, tears burning
her eyes as fear swirled through her mind. She didn't
know when or how, but she found herself in Will's arms.
He held her and she could have stayed in his arms forever…but she couldn't let herself be that weak. Sylvie
never wanted to be so fragile. Still, she couldn't find the
strength to step from the comfort he offered at every turn.

Someone knocked.

"Sylvie?" Ashley's muffled voice came through the
door.

Sylvie shrugged away from Will and crossed the
room. She opened the door and let Ashley back in. "You
have to get out of here, Ashley. It's not safe. Someone
tried to kill me and he's here in the house. He was in the
basement. We have to warn Marguerite, too."

Ashley's eyes widened. "How's that possible? There
are security measures in place here. The bodyguard was
just an added layer of protection."

"Because it's Damon who hired him." Sylvie struggled to say the words. "He's part of it."

"You can't mean that, Sylvie." Ashley appeared
stricken. "I can't believe it."

"My mother says as much in her letter. And you
said she was scared. Who else would she have to fear?"

Hands trembling, Ashley held her cell at her ear.
"I'll get Jeffers up here. He's in charge of security at
the house. And we'll call the police. But your stepfather
has a bodyguard on the way for you. Oh." She shook

her head as realization struck. "Why would you trust a bodyguard if you think your stepfather is trying to kill you? For that matter, can we trust Jeffers?"

Ashley spoke to someone on the cell, explaining there was an intruder in the house. Then she turned her attention back to them. "I know how much he loves you, and I don't believe it's true that he'd try to hurt you. There must be some mistake. Someone else must be behind these attacks. But Sylvie, get out of the house now and call the police. I'll wait for Jeffers and we'll look at the security cameras." Ashley shooed at them. "Go on…"

"But you're not safe, either, if you stay here and work for a murderer."

"Don't worry. I've taken a position with another company. This is my last week to work for Damon, if that will ease your mind."

Will stepped close to Sylvie. "We're leaving *now*."

"Go, Sylvie. Get out of here." Ashley opened the door for them, urging them to hurry. "I'm calling the police, too."

"In her letter, my mother said she couldn't trust the police here, so neither should you."

Sylvie should let her read the letter, but she held it close.

Ashley pursed her lips. She took Sylvie's hand. "Go and be safe. I'll do what I can from here. I know you resent him for the struggle he and your mother had, but Damon is a good man. Trust your heart. He loves you. He wouldn't try to kill you."

An emotion flashed behind Ashley's eyes. What was it? Love? Hate? Was Ashley in love with Damon Masters? Was she his most recent lover? Sylvie didn't have time to ask her, or to consider it further when Will pulled her through the door.

SIXTEEN

Pulse pounding, Will led her down the hallway, watching every corner, every angle, knowing that the man after her could jump out and kill her at any moment. They bounded down the steps, and after a cautious peek through the front door into the waning light of day, Will ushered Sylvie through.

"We should have waited for Jeffers to see us out, Will." Sylvie rushed with him down the steps and to the circular drive.

Except...

"Where's the car?" Hands on his hips, Will glanced around, searching the property. "Where's the Camaro?"

Dread twisted his insides. How would he get her out of here?

"Who would have moved it?" Sylvie asked.

"I think we both know the answer to that. Diverman, of course. And he left us without an escape. Now we're trapped, unless we want to hike out on foot."

"Just relax. We can use one of Damon's cars. Let's head to the garage."

Of course. Why hadn't Will thought of that? Damon Masters would have more than a helicopter for his transportation. Will kept the sarcasm to himself. *And where was that Camaro? In the garage?*

There was no telling what—or who—else they'd find in the garage. Will fingered the knife, pulled it from his pocket. It wasn't much, but it was something.

Sylvie led him around to the side of the house with its innumerable overhangs, and wait…a waterfall? Really? Water trickled over stones, pouring from a peaceful pond, and the brook journeyed to meet the river, he assumed.

Will wasn't sure this was the answer. "Where's the garage, Sylvie? Maybe we should hike out, after all. Get to the nearest town and get help."

What he wouldn't give to have a small plane sitting on an airstrip right over there to the left of that helipad.

The helicopter!

A man—Diverman—stepped from behind a dark corner and grabbed Sylvie. She screamed. Will started to lunge but the man instantly pressed his gun at her temple. "You've caused me more trouble than this ever should have been."

"Let her go." Adrenaline pumped through Will, blurring his vision with rage.

Diverman laughed. "I don't think so. You're not slipping out of my hands this time."

"Who…who hired you?" Sylvie tried to sound strong and unafraid, but her words crackled with fear. "Damon?"

"Wouldn't you like to know?"

"You're not going to kill me. You can't kill me here."

"You're wrong about that. I *can* kill you here. Right here and now and nobody would *ever* find you. Same as they haven't found your mother. I'll make sure you join her since I have to go back there anyway, to search for that thumb drive. All because you couldn't just let her rest in peace."

Will couldn't lunge at Diverman or he would make good on his word. By the look in his eyes as they took Will in, the man was ready to kill, and he would start with Will. Get him out of the way. While he shot Will, that might be Sylvie's chance to escape, but Will needed to harm him, to maim him so she'd have a fighting chance of getting away.

He'd dropped the brick long ago, but he couldn't have thrown it and made a difference. But the knife… the knife was made for moments like these.

In an instant, the man turned the weapon on Will, who flicked the knife in a straight throw, piercing Diverman's gun hand. Screams erupted from both Sylvie and Diverman, as pain burned Will's shoulder. The man grappled for his weapon with his other hand, and Sylvie rushed to Will. He wasn't in a position to fight Diverman, who still had a gun, but at least his aim would be off, his left hand obviously unwieldy at best.

"Come on!" Will grabbed Sylvie and they sprinted away from the house and garage and across the lawn.

"Are you okay, Will? He shot you!"

"No time to worry about that now. Just a scratch."

"But the garage is back that way."

"Right, and so is Diverman. I have a better idea." Breathing hard now, he dragged her to the helipad.

"You've got to be kidding me."

Will wouldn't stop running until he made it to the helicopter. But Sylvie dug in her feet, and that brought Will to a halt. He turned. "What are you doing? We have to get out of here."

"We can't steal the helicopter. What if he needs it?"

Had she lost her mind? "We're not stealing it, we're borrowing it. It belongs to your stepfather, remember? We were already planning to take one of his cars—this isn't that much worse. Desperate times call for desperate measures."

"What about the pilot? We could ask him to fly us out?" Her shoulders drooped. "You're right. He could be involved."

"Diverman is coming, Sylvie. No time."

She didn't trust Will to fly with his injury. That was understandable. Will climbed in but noticed Sylvie hadn't followed suit. He jumped out and ran around to her side. "What are you waiting for? Let's get out of here before we miss our chance. You hate to fly. I haven't forgotten, but we have no choice." Will rubbed her shoulders. "Come on, Sylvie. You promised me you would fly again. This is the time to do it."

She squinted at him. "You sure you can fly this thing?"

"As good of a bush pilot as I am, I'm even better in a helicopter." An exaggeration, but desperate times…

Will spotted a figure in the shadows running toward them from the house. "I think our time is up. Get in."

After he made sure Sylvie was in the helicopter, Will ran around and climbed inside. Glanced at the console, taking it in quickly. He didn't have time to go through a flight checklist. It was now or never, and he'd rather take his chance that the helicopter was already prepped. At least the engine was still warm.

Once they were in the air, Will glanced down to see the man running after them, clenching his hand beneath his arm, and firing his weapon off—way off. Will could almost smile at that, but he needed to focus on getting them out of range. He didn't want to risk a random bullet catching them. He and Sylvie had theorized that her death was supposed to look like an accident, especially if it were to happen at her stepfather's house. So much for theories. Diverman had become desperate to fulfill his deadly contract or else.

Will had been through this twice now—someone shooting at him while he was airborne. Shooting at Sylvie, rather, and that was two times too many. He was ready to resolve this, but how? Where to go next?

"Are you okay? He shot you."

"The bullet grazed me, that's all."

"I'm sorry that I hesitated. I know that could have cost our lives. It's just that… I never told you why I hate to fly. You never asked. You probably assumed it was just a phobia, but there's more to it."

"I'm listening."

"I attended a private school in Seattle, growing up. Living secluded as we were here, that meant a daily ride in the helicopter to and from school. That drew too much attention to me. Even though most of the students came from wealthy families, I was embarrassed. But then, one day while on the way to pick me up, for reasons unknown, the helicopter crashed and killed the pilot. A man I had come to love and trust. Not to mention I, too, could have been on the helicopter. I guess the whole incident traumatized me. But after that, I had a tutor at the house. She was a Christian. Faith had never really been part of my life before that. Mom started taking me to a tiny church in town just up the road. Then I went off to college and followed my dreams. I haven't flown since then…except with you that day when you saved my life."

Will cleared the thick emotion from his throat. "I'm sorry to hear that happened, Sylvie. Real sorry." And now, of course, she could add her mother's death to the list of reasons to be afraid of flying. He had his own morbid story but they had other issues to discuss. Will flew low and radioed the flight tower in Bellingham, hoping to land there. *And where was that Camaro?* His stomach tightened as he thought about what they'd been through. What they must still face.

"Tell me about the letter now."

Sylvie pulled it from her purse, and using a small map light, read the letter to him, her voice shaking. The letter revealed much and yet remained cryptic. They needed a plan and quick.

"So what's next, then, Sylvie? Since your mother didn't feel safe going to the police, should we follow her intended path and head to Mountain Cove? Nobody would expect us to go there, would they? We could show Chief Winters the letter, or get back in touch with the state troopers."

When she didn't answer, he found her staring out the window. She always liked to think before she spoke. He had learned that much about her. She must be more than confused, as was he, about whether Damon Masters was involved or not, considering Ashley had tried to convince them otherwise. The woman sounded emotionally attached to her boss, though—in a way that might color her opinion. Had Sylvie caught on to that? What was Ashley's role in this, if any, other than as assistant? Will had a lot of questions, but he needed time to think. To clear his head.

This was moving too fast.

"No."

"What?"

"We can't talk to anyone until we have that thumb drive in hand." She shifted in her seat, turning to look at him. "Don't you see? Nothing can be proved, even if we go to the police, without the solid evidence on that drive. That's why they wanted to kill me, so that I wouldn't find it. They knew I was getting too close. If they'd succeeded, who knows if anyone would have found me for months or even years, if ever?"

Just like their mothers in the downed plane. Will frowned, watching the airport lights grow near. "If they wanted the thumb drive they would have made the dive and searched for it already."

"No. They haven't found the plane. Only knew that I was diving in the general vicinity where they expected it would have gone down. I haven't found it yet, either, but I spotted something suspicious—something that looked like it could have been part of the plane, just before Diverman attacked. Think about it, Will. Diverman is the same one we've seen everywhere, trying to kill me. He and Rifleman. He hasn't been diving after the thumb drive or else he wouldn't have had time to follow us. And it's doubtful he, or whoever is calling the shots, wants to bring in yet another person just to dive for that plane. The fewer who know about the thumb drive and information worth millions, the better. Diverman's only mission, at the time, was to kill me there. Make it look like an accident, but he failed. He told us he doesn't have the drive yet—that means we still have a chance to get there first. We have to go

back. We know what we're looking for this time, and
it's about much more than finding my mother."

Will thought he heard tears wrapped around desperation in her voice.

"We have to get justice for them, Will. And we might
just be running out of time to do that. We have to go
back and get the thumb drive before someone beats us
to it. I have a feeling Diverman knows that, too. We
have to beat him there. We have to find that plane so
we can end this once and for all. Our lives are on the
line here. I'm not going to trust anyone else with them."

Will didn't respond while he landed the helicopter.
He grabbed the first aid kit. They jumped out and he
grabbed her hand and they ran. Seemed like they were
always running. Sylvie was always behind him. What
would life feel like once it returned to normal and he
and Sylvie were no longer running for their lives?

He led her into the airport terminal. Will took care
of his wound in the restroom. Fortunately, it wasn't
more than a graze, just as he thought. That could have
been so much worse. He'd never discount what his
knife-throwing skills could accomplish. Finished with
dressing the wound, Will hurried out and found Sylvie
waiting for him, then pulled her into a secluded corner.
She stared up at him in surprise, her mouth half open as
if she wanted to say something, then she shut it.

Now. Will was ready to respond to her pronouncement. "Let me get this straight. You want to go back to
where this all started. Where a diver tried to kill you.
And look for the plane?"

She shook her head. "You heard me right."

"You're asking me to dive?" Didn't she remember

the part where he told her he hadn't been diving since the diving accident that killed his father?

His throat tightened up at the thought. He always panicked anyway, breathing too hard and fast. The wide-open sky was more to his liking. Why did their mothers' plane have to sink?

"You don't have to, but I was sort of hoping you would. You mentioned diving with your father before, so I assumed you're certified. You've come this far with me, even though I didn't think I needed your help. But I know now that I was wrong. This time I'm *asking* for your help. I can't trust anyone else. And like you keep telling me, we're in this together."

Her lips puckered a little. She couldn't know what she was doing to him. Even he didn't understand the power she had over him. He wanted to wrap her in his arms, protect her from the world. Whisk her away if he could.

And he wanted to kiss her. The deep ache of it nearly overcame him. Will steeled himself against the crazy feelings stirring inside. He couldn't do this to himself. But he was big enough to shove his fear of getting entangled with her out of the way to help her.

Despite his warning thoughts, he leaned closer. Another centimeter or two and their lips could meet. Sylvie closed her eyes, like she expected, even wanted, him to kiss her.

He drew in the essence of her. He could live on that for months. The thought shocked him back to his senses and he took a step back. Her eyes popped open. Flashed with emotion. What? Disappointment?

Will should take another step back. Put more distance between them. He stood close to her as though this was an intimate conversation. True, he didn't want anyone overhearing their discussion. Deep down, though, he knew it was more than that. His heart betrayed him. Hand pressed against the wall, he barricaded Sylvie from the prying eyes in the terminal.

Just to be clear, he leaned close again and spoke in hushed, but deliberate tones.

"I'll dive with you, Sylvie. I wouldn't let you go alone. You have to know that by now. But we're doing this because time is of the essence. And if I'm going to dive that means you're going to fly. We don't have time for the ferry. You're going to get on a plane with me. I have contacts here, so I can probably get us a deal on a plane rental. It'll be faster than flying commercial since I doubt we can get a flight out until early morning anyway." Will got on his cell to begin his search. Since it was night, he'd have to file a flight plan to fly IFR, using Instrument Flight Rules instead of visual, which is how he usually flew in the bush. No scud running tonight. "We can be in Mountain Cove in a few hours. Get the diving gear we need and I know where we can get a boat. Do we have a deal?"

She paled slightly, but stood taller. Her chest rose with her intake of breath. "Deal."

That was the Sylvie he knew and had come to care deeply about. Wait. Care deeply about?

"So by this time tomorrow it could be over." But it was going to be a long night getting there.

Will's cheeks ballooned then he blew out a breath. By tomorrow his credit card could be maxed out, and they would either have succeeded in finding the plane and the thumb drive or they would have failed. He'd know if he had survived diving, but he doubted his heart would survive Sylvie.

So much for being a survivor.

Here she was, flying with Will again, and in a bush plane, no less. Prop planes were the worst, if you asked her. The little plane rocked and rolled. Puddle-jumpers, they called them, and for good reason. She wished she had it to do over again and try to renegotiate with Will. Her stomach lurched.

Oh, Lord, what was I thinking? Please let us live. Let us survive this.

Hadn't that been her prayer for days now? But at least it seemed to be working so far.

The whir of the props droned on, and the flashing strobe on the wings competed with the flicker of lights below. Eventually, the small plane drifted over a completely dark abyss. They were over water.

"At least they predicted good weather," she said.

"I always plan it being worse than the forecast."

"Is that experience talking?"

"Sure is," Will said. "You might as well get some sleep. It'll be a few hours, and with what we have planned, you need your rest."

"I don't think I can sleep. This ride isn't exactly smooth."

"All you have to do is let go. Just let go and trust me. I know that might be hard to do considering our last trip, but those were extenuating circumstances, and I *did* land the plane. I *did* get us to our destination."

Sylvie wasn't sure that reminder eased her fears. But she certainly couldn't change the outcome by worrying the whole flight. Maybe she should trust Will. Maybe she should let go and trust God. It was time she gave up trying to control the outcome and believe that she really could trust this entire situation—not just flying, but the search for the truth—to God.

"Will you need to stop to fuel up?"

"Yep. But I know my way around, remember? Leave this to me."

"I trust you, Will. I know you'll get us there." It felt good and right to say the words to someone. To say those words to Will. She could sense it pleased him, too. She wanted to pull her gaze from the window. Wanted to look at him, but was afraid of what that would do to her at that moment. Afraid of just how much trust she'd put in one person. The emotions he stirred in her battled against her resolve never to trust anyone, especially men, when it came to matters of the heart.

But who was she kidding? She had nothing to worry about. Once this was over and the killers were imprisoned, they would each go their separate ways.

Will would go back to his bush-piloting business.

Sylvie back to her scuba diving.

Even if she trusted him with her heart, could trust him to be true to a committed relationship, they were just too different to make it work. She closed her eyes, willing herself to drift to sleep amid tumultuous emotions the letter had stirred, confirming the very thing she'd wanted to disprove—that her stepfather had killed her mother. That he was not only guilty of orchestrating her murder, but also of trying to kill Sylvie to prevent her from discovering the truth.

She thought she was going to be sick. How could she sleep with so much riding on her finding the thumb drive? With so much twisting around her throat and choking off her air.

And at that moment she struggled to breathe. She was strapped in the seat belt and couldn't free herself as Will's plane sank deeper and deeper. Bubbles escaped her nose and she looked to her left. Will was in his seat, his eyes closed.

"Will!" She shook him but he wouldn't wake up.

She couldn't save him if she couldn't free herself first. Finally, she unlatched the seat belt—only her stepfather was on the other side of Will pulling him out of the plane. Then her mother was in the water. Alive and in the water, fighting Damon.

Sylvie's lungs screamed. She had to get air or she would drown. She fought her way to the surface, but Diverman was always there pulling her back down. She fought him but she'd already been beneath the water's surface far too long.

She would die. They would all die.

Releasing her last breath, she yelled into the water.

Sylvie fought the arms that gripped her. Shook her until her eyes opened. Will's face filled her vision as she sucked in a breath. But she was back in her seat, strapped in. Sylvie fought to disentangle herself from the straps.

"Sylvie, calm down." Will tightened his grip. "It's all right. You were dreaming."

Her brain finally caught up with her panic and she slowed her breathing. "I thought I was drowning. We crashed again, in the water like before. Only this time we sank."

"Well, then, you'll be glad to know that we have safely landed in Mountain Cove."

She relaxed back in the seat. "I don't want to fly again, Will. Don't make me."

"Your dream was about drowning not flying." He tucked in his chin. "Maybe we shouldn't dive tomorrow."

"Tomorrow?" Oh, that's right. It was the middle of the night. "I forgot we have to wait until morning to get the equipment we need."

Sylvie feared she wouldn't make it to the downed plane first. She had the keen sense she was on a race to the thumb drive, if she already wasn't too late. She was on a mad rush to save her own life by destroying her stepfather's.

"Relax, Sylvie. There's virtually no way Diverman can beat us there. I've made a lot of friends in this business. I do favors for them. They do favors for me. A few phone calls should get us into the local dive shop to get the gear we need."

"But I don't want to involve anyone else in this. I don't want anyone else to get hurt. No one can know what we're doing. That is, until it's over."

"Don't worry. If people want me to keep their secrets, as in some of the outrageous packages I've picked up or delivered, then they'll have to keep mine. I think we should let your half siblings know what we're doing, though. Let Chief Winters know, too."

"Only if you think he won't try to stop me, or tell me not to go." By the look on Will's face, he couldn't promise her that. "Will, you understand everything is at stake here. Our *lives* are at stake if we don't find the one thing that can put these men away. We can't let them get to the evidence first. They won't wait for Chief Winters or the AST to act."

Will frowned and exited the plane.

Exhaustion and guilt weighed heavily on Sylvie and she almost succumbed to the paralyzing effects, remaining in the seat until Will opened the door on her side and assisted her out. The dream—more of a nightmare—had zapped her reserves.

Will steadied her on her feet. Would she be stronger if Will wasn't here to help her? Was she leaning on him too much, something she never wanted to do? She wasn't sure, but she decided to simply be grateful. What kind of person went to the lengths he'd gone to help her? But it was about his mother, too. She couldn't forget that. And he wasn't helping just her. He was helping himself, as well.

Would they even survive?

SEVENTEEN

The sunrise eclipsed the fears that had driven him mad during the night and finally awakened him. He steered the cruiser over the water to the remote part of southeast Alaska where he'd first come across Sylvie, running for her life.

He almost turned the boat around a thousand times. Finding the information that would answer their questions and set them both free could also end their lives if their attackers found them here again. But Sylvie would never stop.

And neither would he.

It wasn't enough that they had the letter her mother had written. It wasn't enough that someone had tried to kill her and they could identify the assailants if they were ever caught. Convincing the authorities to take action would take too long. They needed the thumb drive in their hands, though that hadn't done her mother much good.

Awestruck at the golden sunrise shimmering off the clouds and splaying across the water, Will allowed himself to soak up the peace he always felt at seeing it— and as wonderful as it was here on the boat and open water, it was even more majestic from the air on an early-morning flight.

They were almost to the island, and the channel, where it had started. Will stopped the boat and let it drift while he soaked up the moment. Since he'd flown them to Mountain Cove, he'd let her drive the boat a few hours, and she'd made good time even driving slower to compensate for boating at night. But he hadn't been able to sleep more than a couple of hours and had soon relieved her at the helm. She'd fallen asleep and he'd let her rest a little longer.

He wanted to be sure they were completely alone before they made the dive of their lives.

Then he sensed Sylvie's light-footed approach. When she stood silently next to him, he suspected she wasn't contemplating her next words this time, but instead basked in the glory of dawn, as well.

After everything they had been through together— facing death head-on—Will couldn't help himself. He didn't fight it this time, or berate himself, but did what was only natural and slid his arm around her waist.

Sylvie leaned into him as though there was something more between them. Will knew there couldn't be. He sensed that he and Sylvie were in agreement on that. Then what was going on? Was she as confused as he was?

He couldn't deny there was more between them, more than a physical connection, and there was definitely chemistry. As he held her close, watching the sunrise, Will thought Sylvie could be the one to help him forget the past.

But no, that was wrong. Will didn't want to forget the past. Keeping the past, carrying it around with him, was just the protection he needed. That way, he would never again get hurt.

Except equally as painful was the thought of extricating himself from his involvement with Sylvie. He didn't want to do that, either, but the next few hours would be all or nothing for them both.

Bile rose in his throat so that he could no longer ignore the fear he'd tried to push down.

Sylvie stiffened and inched away. "Listen, Will. You don't need to dive with me, okay? I'm an instructor, a master diver, so I do this all the time. And I've been on search and rescue recoveries."

Will heard what she did not say about finding the victims of a downed plane. Did he really want to see his mother that way—after two months underwater? He shoved those thoughts aside. "I'm going, Sylvie. I'll admit, it's been a while, but it's like riding a bike. And—" Will reached up and brushed a strand of her hair back "—I trust you to lead the way. I'm not letting you go alone."

"But someone needs to watch the boat to make sure that the same thing doesn't happen again."

"If Diverman shows up on his boat, I don't want you down there alone. We do this together. If it comes to that, we'll escape together. You need someone to watch your back down there where it matters most."

Will eyed the horizon, hoping the backup he'd called for would come in time. He hadn't wanted to alert Sylvie to his actions because knowing her, she'd lose Will and attempt to go it alone, believing she was protecting him and any others from getting hurt.

While securing their diving equipment and boat, even though it was during odd hours of the night, Will had texted both David Warren and Chief Winters, informing them of their actions, and that they had no time to delay.

He couldn't live with himself if something happened to her and no one knew where they were, if no help came in time to save her. Maybe help wouldn't be necessary. There were no guarantees this dive would lead them to the plane or the thumb drive, and he could be calling in friends for nothing. But there were no guarantees Will's backup would show up in time to help, if needed, either.

"We should get going. I'll circle the island and make sure we're well alone before we dive." Will steered the boat around the island, watching in the distance for other boats. For the enemy. He'd considered taking a floatplane here. It would have been faster, but cumbersome to get into the dry suits, and they needed the boat to warm up after diving in the cold water. Needed a warm shower. It wasn't practical or safe to stay long in these cold waters, even with the proper gear.

"You never told me what happened to you. Why you no longer dive. You said your father died?"

He took his time to answer, steering toward the island, scanning the horizon. Sylvie stood next to him, peering through binoculars. For just a second he squeezed his eyes shut, and that was all it took. Visions of his father slammed him.

"Will?"

"I'm getting to it."

He shook his head and focused. He had to stay on task here.

"Okay, I'm sorry I asked. If you don't want to talk about it, maybe now isn't the time."

"I'm good." Will punched it, speeding around the island. Searching the area for any suspicious activity. Someone waiting for them. Like Sylvie, he sensed they were in a race against the clock.

"My father loved to fly and brought Mom out here from Montana to build a bush pilot business. He also loved to climb and dive, and he served as a volunteer search and rescue diver, too." Like Sylvie. His father had been a lot like Sylvie. He didn't look at her, though, just watched the water as he spoke. "He was on a re-covery dive. A sunken vessel and…there were bodies to recover."

Will wasn't sure this was the time to talk about it, after all.

"He was only forty-five when he died. He was on a recovery dive that was supposed to be a bounce dive. Two hundred feet."

"Deep and cold." Sylvie nodded her understanding.

"Did the martini effect, nitrogen narcosis, get to him? Scramble his brain like he was drunk? Don't know. But at that many atmospheres down, it's easy to see how it could happen. Even experienced as he was, he somehow got trapped in the sunken vessel, and the other divers couldn't find him at first. You can't see your hand, barely a flashlight, in front of your face at that depth. When they found him it was too late. What I can't figure is how someone could be down there in the deep, just to help others and end up dying, too. It doesn't make sense. I never wanted to get in the water again. My only use for it is to land my seaplane."

"I'm so sorry," she said. "Sometimes we can do everything right and people still die."

He didn't want to think about those words with what they were about to face. "We need to talk about this."

"You mean, what it will be like if we actually find the plane? I've been on recoveries, Will, but I admit, the thought of finding my mother twists my insides. When I determined to find the plane, I hadn't any intention of getting closer, only to note the location and report it to the authorities. But then Diverman showed up and changed my game plans. Are you going to be able to handle this?"

"Are you?" he asked. "We're going in for one thing only. The thumb drive that will bring justice for our mothers and end the threat on your life. Our lives. Let's agree that we won't look at the bodies. We'll get the drive and get out."

"And get as far away as we can from this place. I don't want to face off with Diverman or his accomplice again. The next time I see him, I want him and Rifleman to be in a lineup."

Sylvie directed him to where she'd anchored before. They would start there in their search. She checked their tanks and equipment while Will secured the boat. She then gave him a quick review to refresh his skills.

Where was their backup? If anything happened to Sylvie, they would never forgive Will. Not that that would matter. He would likely be dead already because he would give his life to make sure that Sylvie lived. After they layered and geared up to look like aliens, they hung over the port gunwale, ready to drop backward into the water.

This was the only reason he would ever dive again. He had to make sure that Sylvie lived.

* * *

Despite her experience, Sylvie had never been more nervous in her life. She readied the mask, holding it over her head, and eyed Will, searching for any sign of fear in his warm eyes. Any reason at all to object to him coming along. He'd already donned his mask and watched her.

"Ready?" she asked.

"As I'll ever be." He winked then thrust the regulator into his mouth before rolling back into the cold water.

Once she joined him, she watched him for signs of panic then gave him a thumbs-up. He reciprocated. From here on out, they'd have to communicate with hand signals. She dove beneath the surface and flutter-kicked. The water was only about twenty feet deep here but would get deeper. She was aware of the currents and underwater topography in the area.

Will was next to her, and it felt good and right. Side by side they headed toward the place where she'd seen the glint of metal, what could have been the lost plane. *Or part of it.* Sylvie's heart jumped. She didn't like to think about what they might find. She'd been on enough tragic recoveries. Some couldn't stomach it.

Visibility was between thirty and forty feet. She would have preferred eighty but not the colder waters of winter that would provide it. Following the same path she'd taken the first time, she pushed them north from the island, searching for the remnants of that shipwreck turned artificial reef. It was just beyond that reef where she'd seen the glint.

The reef came into view. She lingered there for a moment so she and Will could take in the abundance of sea creatures, starfish and anemones. Will pointed at the giant tube worms. Sylvie wished this could have been a joy dive with Will, exploring the sea life for the simple pleasure of it. She doubted she could ever get Will to join her for something like that. It cost him to come with her as it was.

Their relationship had been forged out of necessity and a common goal. Should she even call it a relationship? Why was she thinking about a long-term future with Will? She shook off the thoughts and surged ahead, but then slowed and turned to check on him. She couldn't forget he hadn't been diving in too many years. Common sense, along with her years as an instructor, warned her he shouldn't be in the water with her. But technically, she could offer no reason, even though there was a great abyss between certified and prepared. He was certified, and that was that.

She had to stop thinking about him and focus on the area she thought she'd spotted part of a plane.

And there it was…the wing of a small plane. Sylvie almost gasped at the sight.

Breathe. Steady and even.

Will's eyes grew wide. Did he recognize the wing? Could this be part of the plane that went down?

He swam closer to examine it. When he glanced back at her, his features were grim behind the mask. He gave a subtle nod. Sylvie took that to mean that this could be the wing from his mother's plane. So it had broken apart on impact? Or…had there been an explosion? Was that what caused the crash?

Sylvie couldn't stand to think of that possibility, or of what they might find.

Of what they wouldn't find.

The wing was here, but the plane could be much

farther, and could be spread in pieces. She would look for a scatter pattern. If the fuselage wasn't intact, that meant they might never find the bodies.

Or the thumb drive.

Her heart rate accelerated. Maybe she wasn't the right one for this task, but she and Will were the only ones. She swam forward and floated next to the sheer wall of a deep crevasse. More sea anemones clung to the wall, and down much deeper, eighty feet or so, Sylvie guessed the plane might rest. It could be spread out, or have tumbled a few hundred more feet from the wing.

She thought she might get sick. Throw up. Now wasn't the time to think of her mother's terror. Sylvie couldn't afford to lose it. She couldn't let herself crumple or let racking sobs take over. She steeled herself, imagining this was just another recovery dive. But she'd only thought she had nerves of steel, as Will had said.

She had no choice but to see this through. She glanced at her dive watch, the computer relaying time and temperature, complete with a tissue-loading graph, to reassure her they had time to search and time enough to ascend. Then she signaled to Will.

They were going deeper.

Sylvie guessed at the trajectory and swam toward where the remainder of the plane could rest. Why was the plane here, so far off track, when it had been headed to Mountain Cove?

Sylvie turned to make sure Will followed her and spotted him about ten feet away. Her heart palpitated at the distance between them. They had to stick together. He turned to look at her and then pointed. She glanced to where he gestured, but couldn't see what had drawn his attention. Sylvie swam toward him, planning to close the distance, but he swam ahead of her, leading her on.

Something told her that he'd found the downed plane.

God, I'm not ready for this. Help me!

Will paused and turned back to face her, features pale behind the mask. There was something behind his brown eyes now that was far from warm. Sylvie never wanted to see that look in his eyes again. She closed the distance. Could just make out a small craft cresting on the edge of an even deeper crevasse. The fuselage was intact, but slightly twisted.

I wasn't prepared to see this.

Will grabbed her. Had she been swimming away? He gripped her and tried to convey what he could not say through his gaze. In his eyes she saw understanding and compassion, and that he shared her horror at the situation—but she also saw his conviction that they had to move forward. Their mothers would never get justice if they didn't find the proof inside the plane.

Sylvie had thought she was stronger than this, and though she'd coached Will to breathe through it when they found what they were looking for, he was the steady one.

But they had a reason to be here. And now it was time to get the evidence that would put her stepfather away—the missing piece to tie him to her mother's murder and attempts on Sylvie's life. The pain stabbed at her now like never before.

Could she do this?

Will left her and swam toward the fuselage. He would do it if she couldn't. She followed him. They would do this together. Now they had discovered the plane, they would come back, of course, with an actual dive team and the proper authorities to recover the bodies. Today was just about retrieving one thing.

She was messing with a crime scene, but underwater crime scenes were the most difficult to comb through. If they didn't retrieve the thumb drive now, it would fall into the wrong hands.

The downed craft was eighty feet deep, resting on the precipice of a much deeper sea canyon. Had the plane rocked forward and fallen farther, she and Will would have a much different kind of dive on their hands.

Sylvie wanted—no, needed—to take deep breaths to calm herself, but she couldn't afford that. Decompression sickness was one thing, but a quick glance at her watch told her that they would soon need to head back up. They would likely need to dive again to complete their task.

When they approached the fuselage, Will was the one to swim to the passenger's side of the plane and search. Sylvie had experience, but Will was the one to take charge, and she let him. In fact, she couldn't look. She averted her gaze, looking at the fuselage of the plane, still in one twisted piece, except for jagged edges where the wing had ripped away. What had happened? A small-enough bomb to simply rip off the wing?

Will had wedged himself deeper, searching for the thumb drive. Her mother claimed to have had it on her when she left—the drive the reason she had fled. Sylvie watched intently, aware that the plane might not be stable against the precipice. Was Will paying attention, too? She needed to warn him and swam closer.

From inside the plane he gestured wildly at her.

Will's leg was caught in twisted metal. Caught and bleeding.

EIGHTEEN

Will held it in his gloved hands—the thumb drive that had cost his mother's life. That had cost Sylvie's mother's life. The price had been too high. With the pain shooting through his leg that was somehow snagged on a sheet of twisted metal, the price might still climb higher.

If he couldn't get free before his tank ran out of oxygen, Sylvie could buddy breathe with him, but eventually she would run out of air, too. The terrified look in her eyes didn't help. He wouldn't have thought it—she being a master diver. That showed him the true danger of the situation they were in. If he couldn't get free, she would blame herself for this for the rest of her life.

He tugged and pulled on his leg, but the pain only intensified, and nothing he did helped to get him free.

Sylvie cautioned him. She signaled that too much moving could jar the plane from the precipice. Will brandished his knife. He had to live. If not for himself then for Sylvie's sake, and Snake's sake, and for his mother's sake, to make whoever had killed her pay for what they had done.

He glanced at Sylvie. She quickly masked the look of no hope on her face, but he'd seen it all the same. He thrust the thumb drive at her. That was what she needed more than she needed him. She could finish this for both of them. He glanced at the knife, recalling the story of the man who'd cut off his own arm to escape being stuck between boulders.

Could Will do that? When he looked back at Sylvie she shook her head, terror in her eyes. He could bleed out before they could get to the surface. Attract sharks. And they would soon be out of oxygen.

Out of time.

She reached for him. He pushed her away. How did he get her to leave him behind? Would it be too horrific for her if he pulled off his regulator and let himself drown? Then she couldn't save him and would have the time to save herself.

He shoved the images of his father's underwater death from his mind.

God, I don't want to die! Help me have the courage to live!

He didn't want to die like this! Nor did he want to put Sylvie through this. It was too much, far too much, for her to handle, even someone as strong as Sylvie.

Then he remembered. How could he have forgotten? His mother always carried a crowbar in the plane. He bent and tried to shift, and pain shot through his leg. He pointed to the back, signaling in hopes Sylvie would understand what he needed.

She nodded.

While Sylvie maneuvered into the back of the cockpit, Will kept perfectly still. The last thing he needed was to cause the plane to shift and fall deeper into the ocean, taking them both with it.

Help could not arrive soon enough. Will wondered what was keeping his search and rescue friends. They couldn't know just how at stake Will's life was at the moment.

He steadied his breathing, despite the precarious situation. Even though it was becoming increasingly clear he was about to die. *God, please save Sylvie. Please get her out of here!*

Will had been selfish to encourage her to look for—

Sylvie held the duffel bag. His mother's bag of tools and other necessities in case she found herself stuck somewhere. Will took the bag and tried to open it but the zipper caught. Sylvie whipped her knife around and sliced it open. Will pulled out what he'd needed—a crowbar. They needed leverage.

But more than that, Will would have to use his knife and make an incision to free the piercing metal from his leg, before the leverage would work. His vision blurred. He blinked a few times and then made the cut.

The pain was unbearable. He shut his eyes. Stifled a scream. He thought he would pass out. At least the cold seeping in would bring numbing relief.

Dizziness swept through him. He refocused his efforts. Together, he and Sylvie worked to pry him free, but even free, he wasn't sure he could swim to the surface with a bum leg.

His leg shifted, and Will pushed himself away from the craft. Sylvie's concerned eyes beamed. She dragged him farther from the plane, blood quickly coloring the water, faster than before.

Will didn't have time to worry about sharks—another kind of danger drew his attention first. They'd been sidetracked, their attention on freeing him, and hadn't noticed a different kind of predator waiting to take a bite of them. At first he thought it was the help they'd needed, but then he saw the glint of a knife and the hostile eyes.

* * *

She had the thumb drive in her grip—it could be dried out and the data recovered—but all she really cared about was that Will was free. What did the thumb drive matter, what did any of it matter, if Will died down here? Died while trying to help her? Suddenly, finding justice for their mothers didn't seem so important. Though they needed this evidence to be free from those trying to kill them, her priorities quickly shifted with this new urgency. Will's life was on the line.

All that mattered was getting him to the surface.

She signaled that they should head up now, and she would assist him to the surface.

Except the look on his face told her something was terribly wrong—something more than his injury. Will tried to pull Sylvie with him to the far side of the plane. They needed to ascend. He was losing his focus.

Oh, God, please don't let him die. Will forced her around.

Two divers had approached, and one drew ominously near. Behind the mask Sylvie recognized the eyes.

Ashley?

Diverman floated a few feet away. Was Rifleman, the man from the ferry, manning their boat?

Shock had her gasping for breath. Ashley and Diverman. Of course. They were working for her stepfather. She'd been such an idiot to trust Ashley.

Will urged her to swim away with him, but no way was he going to be able to outswim these two with an injured leg. Ashley reached forward and tried to snag the thumb drive from Sylvie's fingers. She'd forgotten she even held it there. Sylvie yanked her hand out of reach.

Ashley would have to fight for it.

She thrust a knife at Sylvie, who grabbed her wrist and held it tightly. The thumb drive in one hand, and Ashley's wrist in the other, she couldn't grab her diver's knife. In her peripheral vision, she saw Will fighting with Diverman, and holding his own, even with his serious injury, but he wouldn't last long. Sylvie and Will had just enough oxygen left to swim to the surface, cutting their decompression stops short. She needed to end this and now!

When Ashley eased back on the knife to thrust it yet again, Sylvie twisted her wrist back. Ashley reached for Sylvie's regulator hose, but it was too late. She'd dropped her knife and it sank. Ashley and Sylvie locked grips, then, neither able to get free without risk.

She was breathing too hard and fast, using up her oxygen.

Dizziness took hold. *Oh, no! Please, God, help me! Help Will!*

She would never make it to the surface. That was Ashley's plan. Keep her here, hold her down, until she died. In her peripheral vision, she could see that Will was no longer swimming. He floated lifeless in the water. But so did Diverman.

Had he killed for her, like he said he would?

Fury exploded inside Sylvie. Adrenaline surged and she shoved free from Ashley. Swiped at the woman's regulator, her mask, anything to be free so she could save Will. But Diverman roused and swam toward her. She couldn't take them both.

Her heart would split in two if she left Will behind, and yet she had no choices. None whatsoever.

She turned and thrust away from Ashley to make a swim for it. Ashley reached for Sylvie, grabbing her fin and then her leg. She sliced at Ashley with her own knife. Terror filled Sylvie. She couldn't die like this. Then the truth would never come out for any of them.

Ashley ripped the thumb drive from Sylvie's fingers then released her. She and Diverman swam away. Sylvie made for Will. She had to haul him to the surface, take her chances with DCS again. There was no time to worry about stopping. And that was when she saw what had sent Ashley and Diverman away without killing her first.

Divers. More divers were in the water. Obviously they weren't there to help Ashley and her accomplice. The next thing Sylvie knew, one of the divers was with her, sharing his regulator.

Cade Warren, her half brother. Will must have told him about their plan. She'd warned him against that, but now she was grateful.

Other divers surrounded Will and took him away from her. Tears slid down her cheeks and pooled in her mask, but they weren't tears of joy, even though she was grateful the divers had shown up here.

She wouldn't have survived even to get to this point if it hadn't been for Will. He'd saved her too many times, and now he might pay for that with his life. She wasn't sure Will would make it. *Please, God...*

He might already be gone.

Moments later Sylvie found herself on another boat. David Warren and Heidi Callahan helped her remove her gear. She pressed into Heidi's shoulder, cognizant of her half sister's growing belly, and sobbed. She'd thought she was so strong that she could take on the world, all by herself. Take on her stepfather, Damon Masters, an international magnate.

She'd been so wrong.

Helicopter rotors drew her attention, and she watched it heading away.

She slumped and leaned away from Heidi. "Will…"

"He's fortunate Isaiah met us here in the SAR helicopter. They'll get him to the hospital."

Sylvie shook her head, confused. What kind of help had Will requested? He couldn't have known they would need it.

Heidi must have read the question in her eyes. "Isaiah was already in the air, returning from a call-out that didn't require it. He didn't want me to come today since I'm pregnant, but I wasn't going to stay behind. So he did what any overprotective husband would do. He did a flyby." Heidi flattened her lips. "My point is that could save Will's life."

He was already dead, wasn't he? Heidi must have seen the doubt in her eyes and gripped her hands. "Believe, Sylvie. You have to believe. Have some faith. We all made it here in time. Before it was too late."

When Heidi released Sylvie's hands she opened her palms, free from the gloves. "The thumb drive. Ashley took the thumb drive. The whole reason for everything."

"It's all right. You can tell the police everything. We need to get you to the hospital, too. Looks like you have a nasty cut on your arm. You could need the hyperbaric chamber, too."

Sylvie hadn't noticed before, but Ashley had caught her with the knife.

"Let's get you below deck."

"Will and I borrowed a boat from one of his friends." She glanced over.

"We got it, Sylvie." Heidi smiled. "This is what we do."

Sylvie decided to let someone else take control. She

trusted her search-and-rescue half siblings. And she had trusted Will.

Still trusted him. *God, please be with him.*

Sylvie sat on the cushioned sofa below deck, praying for Will. Letting Heidi offer her hot chocolate and comfort her. But her heart and mind refused to be comforted.

Too late, she realized the letter she'd thought had been from her mother Ashley had generated on her own computer. Made it sound like the words her mother would have said. Ashley must have copied her mother's real letter and twisted it to suit her purpose. Addressed it as though her mother had meant to mail it.

It had been a ruse to send Sylvie back to her search for the plane and to find the thumb drive.

All that so that Ashley could have the thumb drive, and dispose of Sylvie and Will at the same time.

Her stepfather and Ashley were working with Diverman and his accomplice, that much was clear. But why had they initially tried to kill Sylvie when she was searching for the plane, if they had wanted her to find it and the thumb drive?

Sylvie pushed back another tear. She didn't care about any of it. The police could figure all of that out. All she cared about was Will. His warm brown eyes and his thick dark hair. His sense of humor. The sacrifices he'd made for her. He had to live.

Without Sylvie, of course. She had caused him far too much trouble and heartache. She would see that Will was alive and well, and then she would disappear from his life.

NINETEEN

Sylvie leaned against the hospital wall outside Will's room, nursing a tepid cup of coffee. He hadn't wanted to dive. But he'd done it for her. Would the guilt ever leave her? Could she ever let go and move on? They'd both been desperate to solve what happened to their mothers. The price had been too high.

If I lose Will...

No. She couldn't think like that. She had to hang on to hope like Heidi said. Sylvie couldn't lose Will. He'd sacrificed everything for her.

At least it hadn't been for nothing. The Alaska State Troopers had apprehended Ashley at the Juneau airport, confiscating the thumb drive containing incriminating evidence, thanks to Chief Winters. Once he'd heard the story he was quick to act, calling in the "state boys," as he'd termed them.

The state police hadn't wanted to share the status of their investigation with Sylvie, although they'd taken her statement, but Chief Winters had kept her informed. She'd been wrong about so much. Misled. Her stomach soured.

The information on the thumb drive turned out to

be trade secrets that Ashley had stolen from Damon Masters's company in order to sell to the highest bidder. Apparently, she already had a buyer, a company competitor, for millions. With that money, she could live her dreams.

Masters Marine Corporation's R&D had been developing a new eco-ship in order to solve fuel-efficiency problems in the shipping industry. That kind of technology would mean everything to a shipping company. A secret worth millions—money Ashley had been able to leverage to get the hired muscle she needed to take out Sylvie's mother, and try to kill Sylvie, as well.

She peered into Will's room to see if the nurse had finished. Sylvie wouldn't leave his side until he woke up from his induced coma, except for when the nurses sent her away.

Pressing her back against the cold wall, the smell of antiseptic accosting her nose, Sylvie squeezed her eyes shut. Damon hadn't been involved in her mother's death, after all. Shame filled her that she'd believed he would have been. When her mother had taken the information from Ashley and realized what she'd found, she was afraid for her life. She'd already been followed and nearly killed. She had to leave and find a safe haven.

When Ashley learned Regina was planning to leave and that she had the thumb drive, she hired a mercenary to take Regina out. He engineered the plane crash, timing it over waters in no-man's land in southeast Alaska. Unfortunately, Ashley was concerned that Regina had shared her secret with Sylvie. Ashley learned through a contact at the diving school that Sylvie was still searching for the plane. That was when her mercenary accomplice rigged trackers on her scuba gear and boat.

As soon as she got near where they suspected the plane had gone down, he was sent to kill her and make it look like an accident.

Like her mother, she would be lost forever.

Since Ashley was Damon's assistant and right-hand woman, she could easily retrieve the information again. Once she sold it, she could leave the country.

Except that Damon had grown increasingly agitated, believing someone was stealing R&D secrets from his company. As a precaution, he locked her out of the system and called the FBI. When Ashley could no longer gain access to the information, she needed to retrieve the thumb drive, after all, and Sylvie was the person to do it, since she believed she'd found the site of the crash. All Sylvie needed was incentive and to know what precisely she was looking for, i.e. a thumb drive. Then she could die in a diving accident, after all.

Problem solved.

So Ashley copied the letter her mother had intended to send, only tweaking it to serve her purposes, and planted the seed. Diverman had wanted to kill Sylvie and Will at her stepfather's house, and he nearly ruined Ashley's new plans.

Sylvie gulped back the rest of the coffee, ignoring the bitter taste.

She should have seen this coming a mile away. Should have seen through Ashley. But Ashley had seemed so genuine. So warm and caring.

The squeak of footfalls, somehow familiar, drew her attention up. One of her newfound siblings? Her heart skipped at the thought.

But then tumbled.

Her stepfather made his way toward her from the elevators. Sylvie fought the need to turn her back on him. How could she face him? She peered at the white sterile floor, waiting for his approach. Hospital staff exited Will's room, so she could finally go back in. But now she had to speak with Damon.

"Sylvie."

She glanced at him. Saw the regret.

"I'm so very sorry about what happened." He cradled her elbow.

In years gone by, she might have gone into his arms to receive a fatherly hug, but so much stood between them now. Even though he was innocent regarding her mother's death and the attacks on Sylvie, he'd still cheated on her mother. Betrayed his family.

She looked away. "Me, too. I'm sorry I thought you were involved. I know that hurt you." More than she would ever know. "Because it hurts me."

"I can't say that I blame you. Things were so volatile and explosive between your mother and me. And then…there was the matter of the affairs. I'm sorry for those, too, and for the hurt I've caused both you and your mother. I'm sorry that I was idiot enough to think I could trust Ashley." Bitterness spiked his last words.

Unsure what to say, Sylvie stared at her feet. She wanted her life back. She wanted those years back spent with a loving stepfather and mother. When she actually *was* his princess. His betrayal had been far-reaching. She'd carried it into adulthood where it had colored the way she looked at others. Damaged her ability to trust men. But she was done with letting their actions affect her life. Their mistakes rob her.

"So what's next?" he asked. "Where do we go from here?"

She gathered the nerve to look him in the eyes. "We take it one day at a time. None of it really matters to me anymore. All that matters is that Will wakes up."

Because somewhere along the way, she'd fallen in love with Will Pierson.

Will's eyes fluttered, squinting open to the dim lighting of a room. His limbs were too heavy, or he was too tired, disconnected, but he couldn't move.

Where am I?

His lids grew heavy and closed again. That was much better. Sleep. He could sleep forever and be okay with that.

But wait...there was something or someone. Some reason he needed to wake up. Except his body wouldn't respond to his commands, and his mind was trapped in the past.

He was only fourteen and learning to fly, taking the controls of the plane for the first time. His dad beamed with pride, and when he landed, he didn't think he could ever have a better day. He'd come home to chocolate chip cookies fresh from the oven. Mom and Dad were working to build up Mountain Cove Air bush piloting services. He could stay here forever with them, and soaked in the rare warm day in Alaska. He didn't want to grow older. No, he didn't want to see the future. He knew what he would face, and the pain was too much, as it rushed in and over him anyway. His father's death, and then his mother's.

But then there was someone else...someone vitally important to him. And he couldn't save her, either. She was going to die because Will had let her down, too.

A flash of light golden brown hair. Athletic body, and strong mind and spirit.

She can't die. No, Will has to die for her, to save her.

And then he could fly with the eagles, riding the winds of heaven.

He jerked; his eyes opened. Pain sliced through his head. Sylvie stood there, looking at him. That was painful, too. Seeing her standing there in his dream. He shut his eyes, shut out the light and the pain and Sylvie. He'd let her down. He couldn't look at her, face her, even though it was a dream.

"Will," she whispered.

He cringed inside, wanted to run away, but he couldn't move. She took his hand in hers and squeezed. And Will, to his surprise, squeezed back.

"Can you hear me?" Again, she whispered, hurt and fear twisting her voice. "I have to tell you something. I can't keep it inside anymore. I know it's crazy. I haven't known you for long, but I'm in love with you."

Will wanted out of this dream. He had to wake up to get away from Sylvie. It was as if she voiced all his fears of loving someone, all he'd run from. She was taking his fear and offering him the one thing he'd ever wanted—someone to love. But he could never admit it, never let it happen. Why was she torturing him?

And then she sniffled. "They told me you couldn't hear me, but I don't believe that's true. I think you can hear me and that's why I'm begging you to please wake up. I love you. I need you. Come back to me."

Sylvie's voice was so sweet, so comforting, Will decided he didn't want the dream to end, after all, but then he realized...*this isn't a dream.* He fought to open his eyes. Hearing her gasp, feeling her breath against his arm, motivated him to try harder. Will turned his face toward the warmth emanating from her body.

This isn't a dream! Wake up! Don't lose her again!

When had she become everything to him? Will's eyes opened and he stared into the most beautiful eyes he'd ever seen. Her smile nearly did him in again. He tried to return it, but wasn't sure his lips so much as cracked the hint of a grin.

"You're awake," she said through tears, and squeezed his hand with both of hers. "Will, you're awake."

"Yes." His voice sounded ancient to his own ears.

"Did you hear me? I mean, could you hear me talking?"

"Yes." Her words had brought him back, he was sure of it. They had saved him. "I heard."

Fear flickered in her gaze. "And?"

Finally, he felt his grin, and he saw it reflected in her response. Wow, he loved her smile. Her strength. Her beauty both inside and out. Her spirit.

"Oh, Will, I'm sorry. I've hit you with all this when you've just woken up." She turned from him, pulled her hands away and called the nurse. "He's awake!"

"Sylvie, wait." He reached for her, but there was no strength in his arms.

She rushed back to him as others came into the room.

"You didn't let me finish. It's your words that brought me back, and they weren't too much. They were just right. I love you, too."

But Sylvie wasn't allowed to respond as the nurse asked him questions, welcomed him back and took his vitals. Just where had he gone that everyone appeared surprised he was back with them? It wasn't as if he'd been dead. The doctor would explain the details, the nurse said, then left him alone with Sylvie.

Images of his dreams crawled over him, leaving the

fear and memories in their wake. The loss, his personal loss, had been too much. Nausea roiled.

"What's the matter?" Sylvie asked.

But Sylvie was here in the flesh. Alive, not dead, as he'd believed. He would move forward. Be grateful for her. But...

"What if love isn't enough? We're too different. I love to fly. And you're not happy if you're not in the water."

The horror of what had happened came rolling back and rammed him. The pain in his leg, fighting the diver, and then he hadn't been able to breathe. The anguish and pain of it and everything went black.

"I don't care about any of that. I just care that you're alive."

"I must be a weak man. I don't think I can ever go diving again. Can you still accept me, love me?" He didn't doubt it, but he had to ask. He had to put it all on the table.

"Isn't that what love is all about? Giving up, sacrificing, for the one you love?"

He nodded, waiting to hear what more she would say.

"I can give it up for you, Will. I don't need to dive. You sacrificed everything for me. There's nothing I wouldn't do for you."

He saw the truth in her eyes. "Well, there's at least one thing we have in common. We're both willing to sacrifice. But I wouldn't ask you to give up something you love."

"Good. Because I'm not giving you up."

* * * * *

Dear Reader,

Thank you for reading *Tailspin*. I hope you enjoyed it. Of all my books, I've had the most fun writing *Tailspin*. Maybe that's because I've always wanted to write a bush pilot story. When I started the Mountain Cove series, I hadn't yet thought of it, but since my character Billy, aka Will, showed up in several books, I realized he needed his own story. Of course Regina's offspring needed to turn up, as well. Several readers have written me wanting to read the long-lost Warren sibling's story. Regarding Sylvie's need for a hyperbaric chamber, as of the writing of this story, the hospital in Juneau had removed its chamber. In the real world, divers in need of one would have to travel to Seattle or Anchorage.

A question readers often ask is what part of myself I put into my stories. After all these years writing, I've finally learned that it's my spiritual journey. Whatever I'm going through while I'm writing is what goes into the book. And guess what? That's by God's design. This is my ministry! Because if I'm going through it, that means others are also going through something similar and can use the encouragement that comes with knowing you're not alone.

Over the course of writing *Tailspin*, I was in a place where I carried far too many burdens, and continued to gather more. My responsibilities continued to grow and I added more by choice, because I have goals and dreams. Things I want to achieve. But life has a way of dumping things you don't want onto the metaphorical plate, as well. To say that I had become depressed and overstressed is an understatement. The stress made me physically ill. As I prayed and sought the Lord, He gave me this verse about eagles.

But they that wait upon the Lord shall renew their strength; they shall mount up with wings as eagles; they shall run, and not be weary; and they shall walk, and not faint.

Isaiah 40:31

After researching about what this could mean, I learned that an eagle's wings are heavy and if it tries to fly on its own energy, it will quickly tire. But an eagle waits on the wind so when it lifts its wings, it can rest as it0 flies. In essence, God wants us to let go of our burdens and give them to Him, and that's when good things start to happen. I know they did for me, when I let go, and they will for you, too. I love to hear from you so please stop by my website to connect at Elizabethgoddard.com. You'll find my Facebook and Twitter links there, too.

Be blessed!
Elizabeth Goddard

REQUEST YOUR FREE BOOKS!
2 FREE RIVETING INSPIRATIONAL NOVELS
PLUS 2 FREE MYSTERY GIFTS

Love Inspired®
SUSPENSE
RIVETING INSPIRATIONAL ROMANCE

SPECIAL EXCERPT FROM

Love Inspired
SUSPENSE

A military medic and a rookie K-9 officer find a connection in the midst of a drug crisis in Desert Valley.

Read on for an excerpt from
TRUTH AND CONSEQUENCES,
the next exciting book in the captivating
K-9 cop miniseries, **ROOKIE K-9 UNIT,**
available May 2016 from Love Inspired Suspense.

"Get out of here. Now."

David Evans glanced up at the man holding a gun on him and then glanced down at the bleeding man lying on the floor of the passenger train. "I'm not leaving. I'm a doctor, and this man needs help."

The gunman who had just stabbed the train attendant glanced at his buddy, agitation obvious as he shuffled sideways on the narrow aisle.

David had seen the whole attack from the doorway of his seat a few feet up the aisle. While the two argued about leaving without the packages of drugs they'd dropped, David had hurried to help the injured man.

But before they got away, the two possible drug couriers had spotted David moving up the aisle.

"You better keep traveling, mister, if you want to live. I'll finish off both of you if either of you talk."

David held his breath and stayed there on his knees while the two men rushed off the train.

"I'm a medic," he told the shocked older man. "I'm going to help you, okay?"

The pale-faced man nodded. "He stabbed me."

"I saw," David said. "Just lie still while I examine you. Help should be on the way."

When he heard sirens, he breathed a sigh of relief.

He'd come here searching for a woman he didn't really know, except in his imagination. But a promise was a promise. He wasn't leaving Desert Valley without finding her.

When he looked up a few minutes later to see a pretty female officer with long blond hair coming toward him, a sleek tan-and-white canine pulling on a leash in front of her, David thought he must be dreaming.

He knew that face. While he sat on the cold train floor holding a bloody shirt to a man who was about to pass out, he looked up and into the vivid blue eyes of the woman he'd traveled here to find. Whitney Godwin was coming to his aid.

Don't miss
TRUTH AND CONSEQUENCES by Lenora Worth,
available May 2016 wherever
Love Inspired® Suspense books and ebooks are sold.

www.LoveInspired.com